The Co-Conspirator's Tale

Ron Jacobs

Fomite

Burlington, Vermont

ISBN-13 9780983206309

Fomite
58 Peru Street
Burlington, VT 05401
www.fomitepress.com

Cover Photo Copyright © 2010 by Steve Johnson
Creative Commons License Attribution - Share Alike 2.0
Author photograph by Hannah Thistle

To the people of Telegraph Avenue

The Facts

After conversations with Porgy Johnson's lawyer (Mariah Callahan), a retired undercover agent (Richard Stevens) for the political and gang wing of the State of California's Bureau of Investigation (CBI), and a friend of Johnson's (Peter Somers), *The Weekly* summarizes the case below.

- June 23. 1979: Street personality Thomas Africa killed by Berkeley Police on Telegraph Avenue.
- December 19, 1979: New People's Liberation Front (NPLF) firebombs Berkeley Police cars in response to the murder of Africa. Three cars destroyed. NPLF claims responsibility in a statement reported by radio station KPFA.
- March 1980: Undercover policewoman Rosie McNamara's body found in Marin County. Apparent homicide and sexual assault. Large amounts of barbiturates found in her bloodstream. Police tell public they are searching for two African-American men.
- April- June 1980: NPLF members go underground. Porgy Johnson becomes prime suspect in murder of McNamara. His name is

put on the FBI's Most Wanted list. He disappears into Mexico. Johnson assumes the identity Esteban Cruz. The other suspect is apparently removed from consideration. According to retired CBI agent Richard Stevens, this individual, referred to as Freedman in defense documents, was known to most of his acquaintances as Ra. He was a long time informant for a number of California police agencies, including the LAPD, CHP, and the Berkeley and Oakland Police departments. Stevens believes to this day that Freedman was the murderer.

• February 17, 2007: *America's Most Wanted* features the murder of Rosie McNamara and the disappearance of the "number one suspect in the case, Porgy Johnson" on its show. Johnson is assumed to still be somewhere in Mexico.

• March 17, 2007: Johnson attends his mother's funeral in Oakland, California. Police arrest him soon afterwards in traffic stop.

• Early April 2007: Attorney Mariah Callahan is assigned to Johnson's case as a public defender. She struggles with the case due to a paucity of information.

• Early May, 2007: Peter Somers, a former friend of Johnson's and other NPLF members, receives letter from Callahan asking for assistance. Somers flies to Berkeley to help out.

• July 23, 2007: During a visit with Johnson, Callahan and other visitors are hastily removed from the Santa Rita Jail grounds after a disturbance breaks out. The disturbance spreads. The facility is calm by morning. Four inmates die during the disturbance. Johnson is one of them.

From an article titled "Death of A Revolutionary" in the *Hunter's Point Weekly,*
September 9, 2007

Late April 2007

Rutland, Vermont. Peter Somers sat in a bar drinking. The Red Sox were playing the Yankees at Fenway. Death continued to make its pointlessness known in Iraq. Washington's surge was underway. Somers had a letter from an address in Oakland regarding a part of his past he thought was dead. The writer wanted him to go out there. Once he got past the fact that the letter had found him, he made plane reservations for Oakland the same day. He wasn't doing anything anyhow. Just quit a job. Made twenty thousand from selling his house. Might as well go to California.

The next day he was at an East Bay property manager's office. He had just rented an apartment in the same building some of his friends had lived in the 1970s. Somers left the rental office and walked four blocks south to the building. It looked pretty much the same. Fresh paint and some new landscaping. The recycling center was still next door and the hospital was up Dwight Way towards Telegraph Ave. The trees were bigger of course, especially the monkey puzzle near the hospital.

Mr. Somers, the letter began. It was on lawyer letterhead. Dated April 15, 2007. A woman lawyer in fact. The office address was on Broadway in Oakland. The letter was written pretty informally for a lawyer.

You do not know me. However, you may recall Porgy Freedom Johnson. I am an attorney serving as a public defender for Mr. Johnson. Mr. Johnson claims to have known you during the period of 1976 until 1980 or thereabouts. More importantly, he tells me that you can testify to his innocence of a murder he is charged with that occurred sometime in the winter of 1979-1980. As Mr. Johnson's attorney, I hope this is the case. Otherwise he will be spending the rest of his life behind bars in one of California's supermax prisons.

Although this letter is not the best forum to explain the entire case, let me summarize how I came to represent Mr. Johnson. As you may or may not know, Mr. Johnson has been living in Mexico for the past 27 years. He had assumed the name of Esteban Cruz and had not been in contact with any law enforcement during that time. However, he recently returned to Oakland to attend his mother's funeral. After the funeral services were over, he was riding in a car with an old acquaintance. The car was pulled over by the Oakland Police Department for expired registration. The police conducted warrant checks on the persons in the car and were ready to let the individuals go with a ticket when one of the individuals said something to the officer. From there, the situation deteriorated. When all was said and done, Mr. Johnson and the others in the car (two males and one female) were booked into Oakland City Jail on charges of failure to obey a lawful order and, in Mr. Johnson's case, a further charge of resisting arrest. All four individuals were incarcerated overnight. During the period of incarceration, Mr. Johnson's data was investigated further and his false name was discovered as was a fugitive warrant for the murder of Rosa McNamara in 1980.

Since Mr. Johnson has no money, I was appointed his attorney by the court. He has been very forthright in his story and I do believe him. However, the nature of the judicial system is less forgiving in 2007 than it was in 1980. Mr. Johnson remains in prison (he was transferred to Alameda County in Santa Rita two days ago). Your name and address is the only positive contact I have been able to make so far in my pursuit of evidence and individuals that would clear Mr. Johnson's name. I hope you can take some time and energy to help facilitate his release.

Sincerely,
Mariah S. Callahan, Esq.

Peter put the letter back in his backpack. He was thirsty for a beer and wondered if the Black & White Liquor Store was still in existence. He left the apartment building and headed down Shattuck to find out. When he entered he was surprised to see that the store had changed very little. The beer might have been in a different place thirty years ago, but the counter was along the same wall. He bought a six pack of Rainier Ale for old time's sake and walked back to the apartment.

The next morning. Time to check in with the attorney. Peter drew in the dry California air as he headed down Telegraph to the Oakland offices of Porgy's lawyer. If he thought purely in terms of climate, he could trace his time since he last was in Berkeley through the eternal damp of the Pacific Northwest to the often bitter cold of Maine. Tired of walking, at 57th Street he decided to wait for the bus. A kid at the bus stop had his iPod playing quite loud. Peter could make out the strains of Elvis Costello's "Allison." That song was all over the radio the first year he was in California. The number 41 bus was a block away. He took it to 23rd and Telegraph.

Continuing his walk from the bus stop down Telegraph to the attorney's office, Peter couldn't help but notice the incredible number of posters calling for protests against the war. Lots of marijuana club symbols, too. Compared to where he had just come from, it was like he was in another country--a country that acknowledged there was a war going on and where pot was essentially legal. He saw some posters supporting the San Francisco 8. Like Porgy, they were black men falsely accused of crimes thirty years ago. Hip hop blasting from most of the cars driving by.

He found the building at the corner of 10th and Broadway quite easily. An older building, it was not far from one of the many corporate attempts to renew Oakland: an office mall with pretentiously monumental steps and lots of glass that would be easy prey for angry Oaklanders should the town's residents ever decide to riot against the wealth that sucked their wallets dry.

He entered the office. Sat down on a couch in the front room. He looked at the *Tribune* sports section. Red Sox win again.

Fall 1976

At the corner of Telegraph Avenue and Dwight Way in Berkeley – the foot of what is commonly known as the Ave – is a little grass-covered triangle. There are a couple trees and a bench or two. After a burrito dinner nearby Lucy and Peter parked themselves on one of the benches. Peter lit up a joint they had just bought from one of the many street dealers. It wasn't more than thirty seconds before two police cruisers pulled up to where they were sitting, their lights blinking. A swarthy fellow got out of one car, followed quickly by another shorter, heavier guy.

"Stand up there, you two," commanded the taller one as he unsheathed his nightstick. Lucy and Peter stood up. "You got any more pot?"

"Like I'm gonna' tell you." Peter laughed.

The cop didn't laugh. "Oh, a smartass. You must be new here."

Peter didn't say anything. Neither did Lucy. The shorter officer began searching Peter's pockets. When he found his passport he handed it to the other cop who went to the car to call in Peter's name and serial number—warrant check. Meanwhile Lucy provided her license to the cops. They waited while their identities were checked.

"Let me tell you something, folks," began the short cop. "Around here we run the show and you'd do a hell of a lot better for yourselves if you stay off this street."

Peter smirked. "And you, you're a dime a dozen. Our boys love to move jerks like you to Santa Rita. So watch your ass." Santa Rita was the county prison. Lucy and Peter headed back to their motel. The next day they spent several hours in People's Park listening to a fellow named Jackson play some decent blues on his guitar while drinking quarts of beer. When the rain started up, they headed into the doorways of Telegraph.

California--Los Angeles, San Francisco gold, hippies and Harry Bridges, psychedelia and sexual freedom, movie stars and swimming pools. Berkeley and Oakland and their past and present of Mario Savio and the Black Panthers, People's Park and the Barb, the A's, Giants, Dodgers, Topanga Canyon and Telegraph Avenue. The golden land of the great frontier. Where Americans have gone for decades to be reborn. The scene at the triangle reminded Peter that California was also the home of Richard Nixon and Ronnie Reagan.

Lucy and Peter spent the first few days in Berkeley walking in the rain looking for work. Meeting folks, making friends and figuring out a means of survival.

Never really cold, the rain was usually unobtrusive except for the occasional downpour. The bus drivers were on strike.

After moving in and out of a variety of cheap hotels and hostels, they ended up in a house located off of Foothill Avenue in East Oakland. The neighborhood was ethnically and culturally mixed although primarily black. A few years before it had been a stronghold of the Black Panther Party. The building was squalid. It was an old Victorian in need of drastic repair. The toilets refused to flush occasionally and the electricity was questionable if not downright dangerous. Some young guy owned it and refused to fix the wiring or the bathrooms. Their roommates were a part-time chemistry professor who was active in the Communist Party and a Vietnam vet who taught taekwon do. The communist knew most of the key activists in the Bay Area. He was one of those guys that organizes a lot of stuff behind the scenes.

Besides looking for work, the two went to a number of concerts and demonstrations. The weather was great after the first couple weeks of rain. Beautiful nights. Things were relatively minimal. Not to say life was easy, but if the so-called finer things of life didn't matter, it was carefree. As long as one made it to the free meal on the days cash was low everything seemed all right.

Late Spring 1978

Peter sat against a tree in the east end of the park sipping on his tall boy of Rainier Ale. He scanned the park and the streets that surrounded three sides of its perimeter for friends. And cops who were all too willing to haul him in for drinking.

This wasn't just any park. It was Peoples Park in Berkeley, California. Home to many battles between the counterculture and law enforcement. An uneasy truce existed nowadays, but police kept a close eye on the small piece of land, always on the lookout for any type of lawbreaking among the sixties leftovers, students, brothers from other parts of the Bay Area, gypsies and petty criminals that made the park their daytime home.

He picked up the day's *San Francisco Chronicle* he had found in the trashcan near Moe's Bookstore and opened it. Some story about the Red Brigades and the dead Aldo Moro. Afghanistan heating up. A quick glance at the baseball box scores to see how the Red Sox were doing. They were 30 and 24, having beat Baltimore the night before. He began to read a piece on some holdup in Daly City when he heard one of the park's denizens call out "six-up." Universal code to let everyone know the cops were coming into the park. Peter crammed his beer in his pack and waited.

The cops began checking IDs at the other end of the park. Peter hoped they would miss him in the bushes. The last time these two cops had confronted him he had ended up in the holding cell in Sproul Hall. No particular reason. The cops just wanted to mess with him. That's even what they had told him. While he was there he heard them questioning a black guy named Porgy about buying LSD. Porgy had told the cops he bought it off a white dude. The cops pointed at Peter in the cell.

"Was he the guy?" asked the short fat one named Dinkins. Peter knew some of the cops' names, even though he generally thought of them as one uniformed mass with lots of guns. Guns and hate. And occasionally stupidity.

Porgy had shook his head no and the cops told him to speak up because the session was being recorded. He then said no loudly. The cops threw him against the desk and told him that that wasn't the answer they wanted. Peter knew the cops wanted to pin something on him ever since the street paper he helped edit exposed the fact that some of them had been stealing pot and money from various street dealers on Telegraph Avenue. What Peter didn't understand was why the cops didn't just ignore it. Instead, their denials had put the item on the front page of the local section of the *Oakland Tribune.*

The cops were busy rousting some guy wearing a backpack. Peter decided to take advantage of the situation. He left the park through the bushes on the west end, then headed south on College and didn't stop walking until he got to the Oakland border. He was supposed to meet somebody by the Art College in an hour anyhow.

It wasn't supposed to be like this. He and Lucy had left Snowdon in late spring 1976 in her car. The trip across the country was one of the best trips he had ever taken. They camped here and there, stopped to visit relatives in Nebraska, caught a couple rock concerts and made love whenever they felt like it. Both of them had fixed it with their jobs back in Snowdon so they could collect unemployment for a few months while they just enjoyed California and each other. Those first couple of months it seemed like they ate acid at least twice a week. Lucy started getting tired of it. When Peter suggested in December that they go on tour with the Grateful Dead in the summer of 1977, Lucy got a job waiting tables at a joint on Shattuck Avenue near the BART station. She told Peter she was heading back east once she got the money together.

Peter was tempted to do the same but he really had

no desire to go back to the place he had been wanting to leave for years. The east coast did nothing for him. The last couple months together were tearful and angry at times and lustfully sweet at others. Both of them knew that their love was stronger than Peter's desire to go back east or Lucy's desire to stay out west. Still, it wasn't enough to keep either of them from doing what they had set their minds to do. The night before she left they danced their asses off to some hillbilly rock band. Then they came home and held each other until Lucy woke up and kissed Peter goodbye. They made love and she left with the smell of their sweat in her hair. That was in April of 1977. Peter still missed her every night that he fell asleep alone on the futon they had shared.

But he was free. It was up to him and only him to decide where he wanted to go and when he wanted to go there. He never did go on tour with the Dead although he saw a couple shows at Winterland where he met a girl from New York who stayed around for a few weeks afterwards. They spent a lot of time smoking weed and making love. It didn't mean much.

Lately he had been dealing a little bit of acid. Not a lot, maybe a few hundred hits a week. He made maybe twenty bucks from every hundred lot he sold. It was enough to keep him in rent money, food and beer. The pot seemed to come free, so he was taken care of. Getting by on getting by.

Early September 1978

It was one of those nights when Peter had no desire to be on the streets. He didn't feel like dealing with cops, other street people, tourists or kids looking for drugs. He picked up a six pack of Mickey's and a pint of Jim Beam at one of the liquor stores on University Avenue. Then he headed down Shattuck towards his place off Alcatraz. On the way, he smoked a joint of some red pot he'd picked up earlier that day. By the time he was at Ashby, he felt pretty good. By the time he was home, he was floating. He went inside the house, locked the door and cracked a beer. There were some tortillas and cheese in the fridge. He could make a couple quesadillas later. As he drank the beer, he looked through his albums. Searching for Bob Marley and the Wailers' *Catch A Fire*. Just as he dropped the needle on the first cut the phone rang.

"Hey," said the voice on the other end. "Is this Peter?"

"Yeah."

"This is Roger, man. I'm in Oakland."

Roger was an old buddy from Silver Spring, Maryland. He'd spent the last couple years in and out of prison and rehab after he got busted for an ounce of cocaine.

"I'm done with rehab, man," Roger explained, as if he were reading Peter's mind. "And I left Maryland for fuckin' ever."

"Cool. Where you at?"

"Oakland bus station," replied Roger. "What's your address? I'll catch a cab."

"Yeah. That would be great. Bring some more beer." Peter gave Roger his address. Roger hung up. It would be nice to see someone from Maryland. It had been a while since Peter had checked in with his friends from anywhere in that state. The last time Peter had seen Roger was the last time he had escaped from rehab. It was at a friend's apartment in Wheaton. Roger consumed a fifth of vodka and a couple dexedrine. Everything was fine until Roger decided he wanted to drive into DC to see an old girlfriend. He left the apartment after everyone else was asleep, found a car in the parking lot, hotwired it and climbed in. He made it about three blocks to Georgia Avenue and then ran into a parked police cruiser. The cop was with a girlfriend in a nearby apartment but came running when he heard the thud of the crash. Roger was so loaded he couldn't figure out how to get out of the car he had stolen and the cop called backup. By the next afternoon, Roger was back in rehab in a locked and padded room.

Peter cracked the seal on the bourbon and took a swallow. He pulled the bong out of the closet, filled it, lit a match and took a hit. The Marley album was playing the last measures of "No Woman, No Cry." He took another hit and leaned back in the room's single chair. He flashed back on the Marley show he had seen right before he left Maryland. The whole show might have lasted about an hour and twenty minutes but the energy expended was equivalent to shows that lasted twice as long. Lucy had stayed in Snowdon to hang out with her family, so he had gone with a couple other friends. Smoked an ounce of some killer red weed with a bunch of Jamaican women studying at Georgetown.

Peter's reverie was interrupted by a knock at the door. He got up to answer it. Roger stood there with a paper sack full of beer.

"Bro!" shouted Roger. "Have a beer." He walked into the house and set down the sack. Then he took off his backpack and took a seat in the chair. Peter handed him the bong and the weed. Roger took a hit. Cracked a beer and took a deep drink. He took another bong hit and leaned back. Peter sat down on the floor and leaned against a wall.

"Man," said Roger. "I am so fuckin' tired. My body feels like a pretzel. After hitchin' from Maryland to somewhere in Iowa I decided to take a Greyhound because it was so goddamn desolate out there in those cornfields. Plus, I've got a pocket full of Desoxyn and figured that sooner or later the cops would harass me. Fortunately, I found some black guy on the bus who traded some valiums for the speed and I slept for most of the bus ride."

"You hungry?" asked Peter. "I got some beans and rice I could heat up."

"No man, I'm good." Roger finished off his first beer and grabbed another. He reached into his pack and pulled out a small bottle like the kind pharmacies use. He opened the top and poured a couple pills in his hand. 'You want some Desoxyn, Peter? They're 15 milligrams."

"Sure, I ain't got nothing going on." Peter took the pill offered to him and swallowed it. He washed it down with a slug of the whiskey.

"Let me have some of that." Roger took the bottle and swallowed deep. "Where's the closest liquor store? I'll go get a fifth since you know this speed will keep us all night and we're gonna' want more liquor."

"It's only a couple blocks away and stays open 'til two so we got time." The album side was finished. Peter got up, selected a Jerry Jeff Walker album and put it on the turntable. He moved the needle to the song "Mississippi You're On My Mind" and dropped the needle on the vinyl. Roger smiled.

So, anyhow," related Roger. "I got this check for ten grand from the government for getting busted back on Mayday. I partied away about a grand of it and then said to myself man get the hell out of Maryland.

Peter's out in California. He could probably use some company."

It was around four in the morning. Roger and Peter were still riding the Desoxyn high and drinking whiskey. The music was turned down but still going. Roger had related his final exit from rehab and from Maryland. Seems that he went back to court and asked to leave rehab. The judge told him his other choice was three months at Seven Locks Prison. Roger signed the papers. Did his three months. When he got out he went back to Wheaton and his parents' house where he found some government forms to fill out. He had been arrested on the Capitol steps with a few thousand other folks during the Mayday antiwar protests in 1971 and was part of a class action suit for false arrest. Six years later the government settled and sent everyone arrested at that place at the same time as Roger a check.

"I want to invest in some acid or something."

"I can introduce you to a guy."

It took a couple phone calls, but Peter had arranged a visit to a friend in Marin. He planned to introduce Roger and let them figure something out. The next day they rented a car and drove up I-80 and over the Richmond Bridge to Marin. They pulled into the driveway. The house was a modest ranch with a couple pieces of furniture in front. Two young looking women were asleep on a couch. They looked like they were around sixteen.

"Man," said Roger. "Those girls are beautiful."

"And probably jail bait," warned Peter. "The guys who live here like them young and this is Marin. Lots of these girls' moms were hippies and runaways and started fucking around when they were fifteen."

They got out of the car. One of the girls woke up and pushed her hair out of her eyes. She smiled at the two men. Peter and Roger smiled back. Roger followed Peter into the house.

"Hey!" yelled Peter. "Anyone home?" He sat down on the closest chair. Roger found a couch and followed suit. The stereo was playing Howlin' Wolf. Roger was a little nervous. Peter was half asleep. A guy who must have weighed close to three hundred pounds appeared from a back room.

"Hey Fats." Peter gave a small wave and stood up. Fats walked over and gave him a hug.

"Hey Peter. How you been?" Peter shrugged. "You guys want some juice or something?" asked Fats.

"I'll have a beer if you got one," said Peter.

"Me too," agreed Roger. Fats went into the kitchen and came back with a couple Millers.

"Thanks, man," said Roger. Peter nodded his thanks.

Fats sat in a big chair. He had a cup of some kind of tea that he was drinking. A couple people were laughing quietly in one of the other rooms in the house. The three men drank their beverages. Ten minutes passed and Fats stood up.

"Let's go for a walk outside." He motioned for Peter and Roger to follow. "I've got to find my cat."

"Sure," said Peter. This was a good time to introduce Roger. He waved his hand towards Roger. "This is Roger. He's a buddy from back East." The two shook hands again. All three men went outside. The temperature had gone up at least five degrees. It was getting pretty warm. The two girls who had been sleeping were throwing a stick that a couple dogs chased after. Fats waved hello and headed towards the back of the property. There were some stables and a small barn there. They were just inside the stables when a small white cat appeared and started rubbing Fats' ankle. Two horses looked at the men as if they expected to be let out. Fats picked up the cat.

"This is China," he said to Roger. They headed back towards the house. Fats held on to the cat. When he got to where the girls were playing with the dogs, he asked them if they could take care of the horses. The girls headed to the stables.

"I know you came here wanting to talk about stuff, guys, but I'm not into it today," said Fats, taking out a joint and lighting it. "You guys are welcome to hang out as long as you want and do whatever. There's a pond over there. It's a little skanky in parts but it's okay for swimming. I'm gonna' go back to sleep." He headed into the house. "Oh yeah, Roger--that's your name-right?" Roger nodded. "If Peter thinks you're cool that works for me. Come on back later this week and we'll talk. Good to see you, Peter."

"Take it easy, Fats." Fats handed Peter the joint and went inside. The girls had the horses out and were riding them. Roger and Peter sat down on the porch and watched. When the joint was finished, they waved to the girls, got in the rental and left.

November 1978

Peter sat with Porgy on a bench in the triangle at the corner of Dwight and Telegraph. The pope was dead. The white smoke had yet to rise from the Vatican chimney. A Berkeley cop car drove by. They were talking with a young Chinese-American woman selling copies of the latest *Revolutionary Worker*. She sold the paper every week at the same time. Peter usually bought a copy but never really talked with her.

"So, the Gang of Four are now the counterrevolutionaries?" Asked Porgy. He stroked his beard.

"No," replied the young woman. "The current government are the capitalist roaders." Porgy offered her a cigarette. She took it and said thanks.

"So, do you think they'll kill Jiang Jang?" asked Peter. "Mao's widow?"

"Only if the Chinese people betray their revolutionary heritage."

"More like if the army continues to take the side of Deng Tsiao Ping," responded Porgy. The same cop car stopped up Dwight near People's Park. The cop on the passenger side got out and walked back towards Telegraph. "Six up, Peter," he said, nodding toward the cop walking their way.

Peter made a mental note of his pockets contents. A pocketknife, a joint and some change. No acid. He looked up at the young woman. "I'll buy one of those papers if you walk with us to the café."

"Thanks. By the way, my name is Huiliang." She crossed Dwight Way with the two men. Peter introduced himself and Porgy. The cop headed down Telegraph in the opposite direction. Peter relaxed. They headed toward the Mediterranean Cafe a block away. Huiliang grabbed a table and set her papers on it. Peter ordered three coffees.

"So you know about the split in China?" began Huiliang.

"Yeah, we been following it some," said Porgy. "Peter here always leaned more to the anarchist side of things, but we both have a lot of respect for some of the things Mao did. He was my political teacher when I was with the Panthers."

"I hate to see the capitalist types take over," said Peter. The coffee came. Huiliang talked about the RCP's recent actions during the US Navy's Fleet Week in San Francisco and the three of them talked about Iran. The Shah was losing control. It looked like he would be leaving unless the US intervened militarily. Huiliang drank her coffee quickly.

"I worked with some Iranian students back east in

'74 and '75," related Peter. "We pulled together a pretty good demo when the Shah came, but some of the Iranians we worked with had to disappear after the fights that broke out between them and the SAVAK agents."

"Those are some mean pigs," nodded Porgy. Huiliang got up to leave.

"I have to go back to San Francisco to work," she told the two men. "Here is my phone number. Thanks for the coffee." She handed Peter a piece of paper with her number on it. "Your name means kind and good," he remembered, recalling a poem he had read somewhere. Huiliang smiled. She gave each of them a quick hug and left. Peter watched her leave and then turned to Porgy.

"I didn't know you were in the Panthers," said Peter.

"Yeah," responded Porgy. "I left during the split. I used to hang with the Panthers over in Germany."

Peter recalled the first time he talked with a Panther. He was at the Zoom Club in downtown Frankfurt getting ready to see some British blues band. Keef Hartley. Peter watched a couple cops come through the door. They weren't the same two he had seen when they were at the triangle. "Me too, man. I worked a lot with a brother over in Germany who was part of the Huey wing. The international people got pissed at him, but it never got real nasty. I'm thinking that over there they needed each other."

"I just got out before the shit got too nasty."

"Turns out most of the disagreement was created

by the fuckin' Feds, anyhow." Peter was referring to the discovery of government spying and dirty tricks that had come to light during the Church hearings a few years earlier.

"Didn't surprise me," said Porgy. "Just pissed me off that we fell for it."

The cops were rousting some street person near the back of the cafe. He was trying to stay calm but the younger cop was pushing him with his stick. All of a sudden, the guy being harassed stood up and grabbed the cop's club. The cop held on. "Leave me the fuck alone!" shouted the guy. The cop standing by called for backup. The manager of the cafe came out from behind the counter.

"Please leave my customer alone," he implored, looking directly at the cop fighting for his nightstick.

"You stay out of this," threatened the other cop as he unbuckled his club from his belt. The manager backed away. Some of the customers began to pick up their belongings to leave. Others moved closer to the table where the confrontation was occurring. Some ignored the entire situation. The street person let go of the nightstick and tried to sit down. One of the counter workers brought over a cup of coffee for him. He took the cup, his hands shaking. Another worker brought over two to-go cups of coffee for the cops. They took the offering, turned and left the cafe.

"Sure is a bullshit way to get a free cup of coffee!" shouted a customer as they walked out the door. Most of the customers grinned. The cops kept walking.

"They'll get that poor guy the next time they catch him alone," said Porgy.

A Week Later

Roger pulled his car into the driveway. Fats' place looked pretty empty. No apparent party going on. No nude teenage girls sunbathing and no horses in the yard. Well, it wasn't really a yard. Just a five acre piece of pasture surrounded by woods but everyone called it a yard. We just can't get away from our suburban up-bringing, laughed Roger remembering a joke Peter liked to make. Maybe Fats was the only one home for a change. It was so much easier to do business when that was the case.

He parked the car at the top of the asphalt and got out. As soon as he closed the door the dogs began to bark. One of them came running out, its tail wagging. He came over to Roger and jumped up on him. Fats was on the porch by now and waved at Roger when he looked up from petting the dog. It looked like Fats had just woke up. He still had on some kind of nightshirt covering his huge girth.

"Hey Fats," yelled Roger. Fats motioned for Roger to come on in. Peter grabbed a backpack from his car and headed towards the door.

"What's goin' on, man?" asked Fats. "Want some coffee or tea?" Peter shook his head no.

"Got some good herb, Fats." Fats went toward the rear of the one story ranch style house. Roger knew the bedrooms were back there, having spent some time with a girl or two on previous visits. He waited for Fats to reappear.

"Cool." Fats was back and had changed into a pair of jeans and a flannel shirt. He was brushing through his curly hair with a jewel-encrusted hairbrush. "Like my brush? I got it from some Indian dude back in '72. Swore he got it from some Indian chieftain on one of his trips to Nepal to buy hash. Nice fuckin' brush."

He handed the brush to Roger who looked it over. "What are those blue stones? Sapphire?"

"Yeah."

"Nice."

Fats took the brush back and sat down on one of the sofas in the room. "The girls are gone for the week. They went somewhere with John on tour. I think he's going up to Oregon and Washington. Kind of nice to have the place to myself for a change."

"It's quieter but you're not nearly as cute as them girls."

"That's okay. I don't want to fuck you neither," laughed Fats. "What you got?"

"Fifty pounds of some kickass Thai stick. A buddy of mine who made some connections over in 'Nam brought it in." Roger took a joint out of his shirt pocket. "Wanna' try some?"

"Fire it up." They smoked the joint and drifted off.

"That's got some O in it, huh?" commented Fats.

"Yeah."

"What you want per pound?" asked Fats. His eyes were half open. A shit-eating grin was spread across his face.

"I was hoping to do a trade." Roger shifted his weight and leaned back on the chair he was sitting. The Thai weed was really kicking in.

"Yeah?"

"I was thinkin' ten pounds for two grams of LSD crystal. We got some people interested in moving some acid out east."

"Let me think about it. I'm inclined to agree but I need a clearer head."

Roger spent the afternoon smoking and sleeping. Then he headed back over the bridge to Richmond. Then down the interstate to Berkeley.

It was dusk. The California sun settled over the San Francisco skyline. Peter watched it from his spot in Berkeley's Aquatic Park. He was drinking wine with an Ojibwa brother named Kicking Bear. The conversation alternated between Kicking Bear's retelling of the 1973 battle of Wounded Knee and the people he was staying with.

"These mother fuckers, Peter," rambled Kicking

Bear. "They're a bunch of college kids with guns. The women are fine but seem to be all over any guy who is black. I've been trying to tell them they need to keep their guns somewheres besides their house 'cause if the cops come they're goners. But they don't listen-- just like most white people. It's like they think they're immune or somethin'."

"That's what they think, Bear," said Peter, "I know. I been livin' among them all my life."

"Anyhow, when I was at Wounded Knee there was a dude named Blackbird who had left his high school over in Germany to come fight with us. I remember him 'cause he brought in a bunch of ammo he got from a cousin of his white mama in St. Paul. He got hit the second night he was there by the marshals and we took him to the infirmary where he stayed for a couple hours. Motherfucker was a fighter."

"Man!" exclaimed Peter. "I know that guy. We did some graffiti stuff together. I remember him talking about getting an early graduation so he could go to Wounded Knee. So he did make it."

"Yeah. Last I heard he was living with an Ojibwa girl making babies and growing vegetables. Not the easiest thing to do on the rez, you know." Kicking Bear lifted the bottle of wine to his mouth and drank. He was getting pretty drunk. When he stood up his weight shifted from top to bottom while he searched for his equilibrium.

"We need more wine, bro. Let's go to that Vietnamese place." Kicking Bear was leaving the park as he said these words. Peter followed. When they got to the Vietnamese-owned convenience store, Peter stayed outside. Kicking Bear wasn't planning on paying for the wine and he didn't want Peter to get busted if he got caught. Peter sat on the sidewalk talking with an old hippie who was spare changing. Ten minutes later Kicking Bear finally came out of the store carrying a gallon of Gallo,

"What the fuck?" said Peter? "Did you pay for it?"

Kicking Bear laughed. "The Vietnamese dude at the register caught me. He was gonna' call the pigs, but I convinced him not to and he gave me the bottle for free as long as I promised not to steal from him no more."

"How the hell...?" Peter and Kicking Bear were on the way back to the park. The hippie who had been spare changing followed.

"When he snagged me I looked at him and asked him how he felt about the US government making war on his land and forcing him to leave it. He thought about it a minute and told me to go. That was it." They saw two carloads of cops near the park. Turning around quickly, they began to go south on Telegraph away from the park. There had to be a quiet alley just over the Oakland line where they could drink.

Kicking Bear, Peter and the old hippie guy, who called himself Mountain Man Bob, were sitting in an abandoned house that Mountain Man had told them about. They were drinking. The gallon was about halfway gone.

"Man," said Peter. "I'm gettin' pretty fuckin' loaded." He felt a little woozy. Reaching under his t-shirt he pulled out a small pouch. "You guys want a hit of acid? I need it to stay awake." Mountain Man took a hit and tossed it in his mouth. Kicking Bear followed. Peter ate two hits himself. The pills were little purple things about the size of half a grain of rice. Purple barrels were the street name. They weren't particularly strong. Mountain Man lit up a joint he had. The bottle continued to pass between the three of them. The first few times, dropping acid really had been the temporary insanity the researchers claimed it to be. Now, it was a mere calisthenics for a part of the brain not utilized too often in daily life.

"Shit. I'm feeling that acid," said Kicking Bear. It had been about half an hour since he had eaten it. Mountain Man and Peter nodded in agreement. "Let's go to the house I'm staying at. There's supposed to be a party."

"They'll let us in?" asked Peter. "I thought they were into security because of their NPLF stuff."

"Fuck 'em. I'll tell them you're with me. That'll be enough for them."

The three men left the abandoned house and headed west towards San Pablo Avenue. It took them about forty minutes to reach the house. The party was in full swing when they entered. Peter looked around, the acid jangling in his mind and enhancing the blue lights in the lamps. There were twenty to thirty people drinking and smoking weed. About half of them were women and about a third were black. Porgy was there. Maybe, thought Peter, this was where he lived. Some other black guy named Ra was romancing a woman Peter knew slightly who was named Rosie. He never knew what to think of either Ra or Rosie. They just gave off a weird vibe. Porgy walked over to the three of them.

"Peter! What's up?" Porgy gave Peter a hug and nodded greetings to Kicking Bear and Mountain Man Bob. "There's beer in the kitchen."

There was a Temptations hits collection on the turntable. When the song "I Wish It Would Rain" came on, Porgy stood on a table and sang along. A couple of the women--one named Turtle and one that Peter thought he heard called Rhiannon--joined him. All three of them took of their shirts. Things got wilder from there. Ra disappeared with a couple of the women. Rosie sat down on a couch and lit a cigarette. Kicking Bear started talking about the SLA. Rosie joined in.

"Bunch of white kids playing with guns," said Kicking Bear. "They should have known better."

"What about Cinque?" Cinque was the black prisoner who was the SLA's so-called leader. He had died

with most of the rest of the group in the police assault on their house in Compton. "He was a brother,"
answered Rosie.

Peter listened. Mountain Man Bob was romancing
one of the women. She was drunker than him. They
kissed some and found a corner.

"I just don't get their purpose," said Peter. "The
feds couldn't have created a better mechanism for di-
viding the left than the SLA. You know the Panthers
think Cinque was a provocateur. His record of col-
laboration with the police goes all the way back to LA
and that narc who helped set up Bunchy Carter and
them--what was his name, Louis Tackwood?"

Rosie shifted uncomfortably. "Are you saying the
SLA were cops?"

"No," said Peter. "But I wonder about who Cinque
was really working for."

"He was working for the revolution!" Her voice was
loud. A couple other folks from the house looked
around. Porgy looked at him, shaking his head slightly
as if he was warning him to drop the topic. Peter
heeded Porgy's warning and looked away, as if something had caught his attention. Rosie had other ideas.

"Are you saying Cinque was a cop?" she insisted.

Peter weighed his words. "I think the SLA was a
setup by some element of COINTELPRO. I don't
know whether Cinque was the link between the police
and the revolutionaries in the SLA, but the Panthers
investigation makes some things pretty clear and draws

some links between Cinque and the California red squads that are hard to discard." Rosie had left the room. She came back with Ra.

"Get out motherfucker." Ra looked at Peter. "And take your hobo friend with you." He looked over at Mountain Man Bob, who was weaving a bit from the wine and sex. "You don't disrespect Cinque in this house. How do I know you're not a cop?" He moved closer to Peter. Kicking Bear looked up from a game of cards he was playing with a couple partygoers. He surmised what was happening and stood up. His size dwarfed Ra, who was easily 6 feet tall and a couple hundred pounds. Ra walked over to Mountain Man Bob and picked him up by his shirt.

"Leave me alone, you fuckin' motherfucker!" shouted Bob.

Kicking Bear looked at Ra. Ra set Mountain Man Bob back down. Bob gathered his pack and headed towards the door. Kicking Bear gathered his stuff. Peter shrugged his shoulders and followed Mountain Man Bob.

"Fuckin' honky motherfuckers," said Ra.

Kicking Bear was in the doorway now. "You guys have a lot to learn about revolution." He left with Peter and Mountain Man Bob.

The Following Morning

Peter looked up. Roger was in the kitchen weighing out some weed. If this trade went through with Fats, Peter would have a quarter gram of LSD crystal to get started on a little dealing of his own. Roger was planning on going back east with Peter's friend Woody to sell the rest of the weed. In addition, Woody had an acid deal all set to go. If he didn't spend all his earnings on junk back east he would finally be able to buy the land he wanted near the Sierras. Then maybe his last and greatest girlfriend would get back together with him. Roger finished up with the scales, packed his weed and left for Marin.

Late December 1978

It was one of those days that sounded like a depressing Bruce Springsteen song. Peter's life was drifting. Not doing much of anything. Drinking too much and wishing he had stayed with Lucy. It was the freakin' drinking that had got him busted. Now he found himself down at Aquatic Park picking up trash with two other guys busted for something or the other. Stupid gig, but better than jail, he figured. He finished off his cup of coffee and threw the empty piece of styrofoam in his knapsack. The supervisor came over to the three of them.

"Mornin' gentlemen," he began. "My name is Jack and if you fill up a bag with trash, I'll let you go and give you credit for all eight hours." He was an old black guy with a Berkeley Sanitation Division worksuit on. "I figure you all are probably here for somethin' that shouldn't be no crime anyhow. So get to it."

Peter and the other two guys took their garbage bags from Jack and grabbed a stick to spear the trash. They headed towards the beach area of the park, picking up trash along the way. Jack's radio said something about Rhodesia now being called Zimbabwe.

"How many hours you got?" A hippie looking guy asked Peter once they got to the parkland by the bay. He looked to be around 18 or so. Blond hair and a scraggly beard. Peter had seen him in the park and at a concert or two. The other guy was a black guy around forty or so.

"Thirty," answered Peter. "What about you?"

"Forty-eight. This is my second day." The black guy stopped.

"I only got eight left." he told Peter and the blond guy. "Had eighty to start out with."

"What for?" asked the blond guy.

"Possession of coke. I figure I got off lucky," the black guy replied. "A couple other brothers I know ended up getting ninety days in Santa Rita."

Peter put out his hand. "My name's Peter." The three men introduced themselves. The blond guy's name was Jesse and the other guy's name was Ronald. They picked up trash and talked. At lunch they turned in their bags, got checked off for eight hours of work by Jack and went into the bushes to smoke a joint. When the joint was finished they went their own ways.

Peter went down to the pier to hang out a little while until his buzz mellowed out. There was a Vietnamese man listening to some Vietnamese music on his cassette player and fishing. Other than him, the pier was empty. Peter walked out to the end and sat down. The salt water sprayed up into his face. Gulls flew around overhead and a few horseshoe crabs lurked in the rocks. There was a pile of fish guts on the rocks about ten feet from where Peter sat. The gulls flew down and grabbed at it while keeping an eye on Peter. It was like they thought he was competing for their grub. The sun felt good.

Peter lay back on the wood of the pier. He closed his eyes. A half hour later he sensed the presence of someone near him. He woke with a start and looked up. There was a cute woman about four feet from where he lay. She was looking intently at him.

"Hi," said Peter. "I guess I nodded off." He smiled. Her blond hair shone in the sun. He couldn't help but notice her little breasts and their erect nipples.

"My name's moonshadow." The girl reached out her hand. Peter shook it.

"I'm Peter."

"Sorry to wake you." moonshadow smiled as she moved a little closer. Peter responded in kind.

"No problem," smiled Peter. "It's like a dream come true. To be awakened by a pretty woman." moonshadow smiled back. "I was just relaxin' after doing some community service in the park for smokin' weed."

"You got busted?" asked moonshadow.

"Yeah. And I copped a plea," said Peter. "My sentence was a couple days of picking up trash in the park. I filled up my bag and the boss man let me go early. So I came out here."

"It's nice here."

"Yeah." Peter was silent. He was trying to figure out how to get to know this girl better. "You want to get high?"

"Yeah." The two stood up and began walking down the pier towards the park. Peter looked in his cigarette pack to make sure he still had one more joint. They found some bushes to hide in and Peter lit up the joint. Although he was little paranoid, Peter decided he would enjoy the moment.

"That was nice," said moonshadow when the joint was through. She leaned over and kissed him. He kissed her back. Soon her long skirt was hiked up and he was inside her.

"I guess that means I like you," whispered moon-shadow when they were done. She pulled down her skirt, brushed back her hair and pushed Peter's out of his face. "Let's go get some food. I have some money. We could get a burrito or something."

Peter and moonshadow left the bushes and walked towards San Pablo. There was a burrito place a block north of the intersection. Peter couldn't believe his luck as the two laughed and talked. He didn't even care that two cops were taking their break at the burrito shop when he and moonshadow walked in.

Peter picked up the wrappers and napkins from the

burritos. He walked over to the trashcan and threw the waste away. moonshadow was right behind him. They left the restaurant and headed south on San Pablo towards Oakland. moonshadow was coming home with him for the night. She had been somewhat elusive when he asked her if she had a place to stay. It seemed like she needed a break from wherever it was that she was staying. That was fine with him. When they got to Ashby Avenue they turned left and headed up towards Peter's place near the BART stop.

"I've seen you in the park and at shows," moonshadow told Peter after he opened the door and sat down on the overstuffed couch that was the sum of his furniture. Albert King on the radio. No mistaking that guitar. She sat down sideways next to him, her legs crossed under her. Peter kicked off his shoes and turned to face her. They began kissing again. Her skin was incredibly smooth and her tongue was warm. It tasted like green chili with a different kind of heat.

"Yeah, I think I've seen you around," responded Peter. "Do you live near People's Park?" He helped her take off her skirt and she crawled onto his legs. She pulled off his shirt and began to kiss his chest.

"No. On San Pablo with a bunch of freaks." Their conversation ended as they moved to the floor, both of them now naked. Peter lit a roach he found in an ashtray and passed it to moonshadow. She drew in the smoke and exhaled it into Peter's mouth.

Peter tried to remember where he knew her from.

It was around 2 AM. Peter was awake. He knew where he had seen moonshadow before. It was at that party with Kicking Bear. Funny, she didn't seem that militant, but then he had just met her. moonshadow felt Peter moving around. She opened her eyes and put her legs around his body.

"Hey," she whispered. Her fingers gently stroked his face. He looked at her and smiled.

"Do you live with those NPLF people?" he asked.

"Yeah. How did you know?" She licked his stomach and smiled.

"I got kicked out of a party there."

"Oh yeah. I remember. That was you, huh?" She was on top of him now. She leaned over and they kissed. "Some of those guys are so fuckin' uptight about that shit."

"How did you end up there?"

"I don't know. It just kind of happened." moonshadow explained. "I was living on the streets for a couple months after me and my last boyfriend split up. He was a hardcore Jersey Deadhead and wanted to go on tour. I was tired of touring plus I was kind of tired of him. He gave me a couple hundred bucks and split. I spent the money the first week on a hotel room and food. Then I was on the streets. I met Rosie at La Peña after some women's meeting and she told me I could crash at her house. Then I just never moved out. I've been there almost eight months now. I didn't even know they were political or kind of connected to the

SLA until Ra brought it up once at a house meeting. Him and Rosie are the most militant talkers. Everybody else wants to do something about how fucked up things are but they seem more concerned with paying rent."

"I guess I won't ever be sleeping at your place then." Peter chuckled and pulled moonshadow towards him.

January 1979

Shah gone. Three thousand marched in the ghettos of Berkeley yelling bring him to trial. Shah in Panama. The march went through the industrial section of the town. Nobody heard and nobody cared. A guy set a trash can on fire and the cops came down on him hard. Almost started a riot right then. One of the march leaders stopped the truck he was driving, went back and pulled him away from the cops. By then a commander type cop had pulled his zealous patrolmen back. The march went on for another mile.

Porgy and Peter sat in Jack's yard sipping on an early morning beer with Jack and Jackson. *London Calling* on the turntable. They had been up most of the night. In between conversations, Jack and Jackson laid down some pretty slick blues grooves on their bass and guitar. Peter met Jackson the first week he and Lucy were in Berkeley and became good friends with him. He was a local fellow whose dad had fathered several children in between his bouts with heroin addiction. Jackson left home when he was thirteen for the Berkeley streets. He picked up his music making ability from his father —who was a musician himself known throughout the Bay Area for his keyboard playing. Jack was a transplant from Los Angeles who studied bass in high school and had played in a few different rock bands before he moved to Berkeley with his girlfriend. He lived in a small cottage off Durant Avenue. Since he and Jackson had met up, they had developed a pretty lively repertoire of tunes and played quite frequently on Telegraph Avenue.

While they sat drinking beers that morning in Jack's yard, a slight drizzle falling on their heads, four cops suddenly appeared.

"Good morning gentlemen." The biggest one said rather sarcastically. It was the same cop who had harassed Lucy and Peter their first night on Telegraph. "Please empty your beers."

"Excuse us," began Jack. "But this is my house and my yard. We can drink beer here if we want."

"Empty them, he said," said one of the other officers, a pudgy, whiny man.

"Get out of my yard," said Jack.

"If you don't empty those beers," said the first cop. "We'll take you in."

"For what?" I asked.

"We'll find something," he replied.

Peter tipped what remained of the beer into his mouth. One of the cops grabbed it and poured the few remaining drops on the wet ground and smiled.

Jackson stood up to go back inside Jack's house when the large officer grabbed his arm. Jackson yanked his arm free and walked away. The police moved aside and after several minutes of conversation amongst themselves, they placed their nightsticks back in their belts and turned and walked away.

February 1979

It had been a while since moonshadow was in Fats' house. Nothing looked any different. She used to hang out there a lot when she was still with her earlier boyfriend named Ben. She had learned to ride horses while waiting for him. He and Fats knew each other from the old days and Ben sold a lot of Fats' acid back east. She was here with Rosie because the collective decided they needed to make some money. They also wanted to do some acid sessions to get closer. moonshadow felt like she should help them out to prove her worth. She contacted Fats. He told her to come over with one other person and he'd fix them up. So here they were. Rosie said she had done acid a few times. She certainly didn't seem to have a problem with smoking the hash that Fats lit up the moment they came in. They sat around listening to music while Fats fed his dogs. Peter's friend Roger was helping him. moonshadow had met him at Peter's the day after she met Peter. She figured he crashed there when she wasn't around. While the men fed the dogs, Rosie told moonshadow she thought Roger was cute. A little stocky for her taste, but still cute.

Dylan's *Desire* album was playing. The second side. "Romance In Durango." Walter Cronkite and all that. moonshadow smiled to herself. Fats walked over and gave her a hug.

"Hey," said Fats. "Long time no see. How you been? How's Ben?"

"You probably know more about Ben than me," said moonshadow. She kissed Fats on the cheek. "He doesn't really talk to me any more. I'm okay." She wasn't pissed off about Ben or anything. It was just one of those relationships that, when it was over, it was over. Ben had moved on and moonshadow had too. She smiled at Fats.

"This is Rosie," said moonshadow. "She lives with me." Rosie shook Fats' hand. He acknowledged her. Roger came over, gave moonshadow a hug and introduced himself to Rosie. They smoked another bowl of hash and listened to Dylan pour his heart out in the song "Sara." When the album was over, moonshadow got up and went outside. She wanted to check out the horses. Rosie stayed indoors hoping to discuss an acid deal. Fats wasted no time.

"So," began Fats. "Are you interested in buying some acid?"

Rosie nodded. "I have a brother in Chicago who can move some stuff."

Fats nodded. "I would do it only through you. I

don't want to meet anyone else."

"I understand." Rosie smiled. Roger was sitting next to her. He offered her a glass of juice.

Fats continued. "What I'll do is give you a few samples and you can check it out or get someone else to do that. Than you can get back to me through moon-shadow."

"She doesn't really want to get involved in dealing," said Rosie. "I think her old boyfriend burned her out on that scene."

"I could be the go-between," volunteered Roger. "If that's okay with both of you." He smiled at Rosie. She smiled back.

"You sure?" asked Fats.

"I think so," answered Roger. "I mean we won't do nothing until I get to know her a little better."

Rosie smiled. She was getting quite a sexual urge for this guy. He turned her on something crazy. "I could go for that."

"How about we go to a show or something tonight or tomorrow? Get to know each other a little?" suggested Roger.

Fats smiled. He got up and went into the kitchen. When he came back in with a sandwich, Roger and Rosie were lightly kissing each other. He cleared his throat and they looked up. Roger went into another room. He and Fats had some business to conduct. Rosie went outside. Ten minutes later, the two men appeared. Rosie was sitting on the porch. Fats sat down next to her. He looked at Rosie.

"Well, then. I guess Roger will let me know what's up then. He has a few hits of the stuff I'm moving right now. You all can use that to check it out."

Rosie nodded. Fats shook her hand and smiled at Roger. They found moonshadow with the horses and told her they were leaving. After getting back to the East Bay, Roger dropped moonshadow off at Peter's house. Rosie followed in her car. While Rosie waited in the car Roger went into the house and gave the acid to Peter. Peter stashed the vials after moonshadow locked the door. Roger parked his car and got into Rosie's.

"Where's Roger going?" asked Peter.

"He and Rosie are going dancing," answered moon-shadow. "They hit it off just like that."

Rosie and Roger were on the Bay Bridge heading towards the Stone. Nick Gravenites was playing there. They parked the car off of Columbus and headed to an Italian restaurant. After a bottle or two of wine and a hearty meal of pasta, they went looking for a hotel. They found one near the wharf and checked in.

Roger closed the door behind them and Rosie grabbed his face. They kissed long and deep. She peeled off her skirt and panties. Then she grabbed his zipper and undid it. Roger's fingers were inside her. She climbed up on him and locked her legs around him. They moved together towards the bed. A few hours later they woke up. It was around nine o'clock.

Still time to go to the show at the Stone. Roger suggested they split a hit of the acid and Rosie agreed. They decided to walk to the club.

Later That Week

It was her brother who made Rosie into what she was today. He left home when she was sixteen and when he came back he wasn't the same at all. She understood that his time in the army was bad. After all, he was part of the last bunch of guys over in Vietnam after everyone in the States thought the American part of the war was over. Reggie was still over there though, killing Vietnamese and hiding it from the press who didn't care that much anyhow. They were more interested in Nixon going down for Watergate. The worst part of it for Rosie was the fact that he got hooked on drugs. When he came back home in the summer of '74 he was, well, just different. He stayed for a month or two and then Dad kicked him out. The next time she saw Reggie was when she started college in Seattle. He showed up at her dorm one morning and told her goodbye. It had been over a year and he looked like hell. He was leaving the country he said. Mexico where heroin was cheap. She fast-forwarded college and finished in three years. Then she got into the undercover police business. Besides her CBI paycheck she was also now on hire to the DEA.

The NPLF was her first assignment for the CBI, but when that girl from Jersey who called herself moonshadow—the deadhead who fell in with this bunch a year ago—brought that LSD crystal into the house Rosie figured out a way to not only meet the supplier everyone called Fats, but also convinced the San Francisco DEA office to give her the assignment surveilling Fats' operation. The girl never knew what she had done by bringing Rosie to Fats' place in Marin—all in the name of revolutionary love.

Rosie knew she had it. These kids were amateurs. She could take them down any time but was waiting. It was the big fish over in Marin that she really wanted to fry. As long as she could keep these kids from blowing anything up or killing a cop, she could keep the rest of the agency off her ass about them. Fats' operation was the operation she wanted to take down. That man probably moved the equivalent of a quarter million hits of acid every two weeks. Big star in her portfolio.

Except she was falling for that guy Roger. And he said he spent a lot of time over there.

June 23, 1979

Channel Four - TV

This morning Berkeley police shot and killed a man they say was wanted for multiple offenses. Thomas Africa was a well known figure to tourists and habitués of the stretch of Telegraph Avenue known as "The Ave." According to police, Africa ignored their command to pull over the van he was driving this morning around 7 AM. Instead, say police, Africa sped up and tried to outrun the two cruisers behind him. Police say they commanded Africa to pull over twice more and then shot out the rear tires to his van one block from the intersection of Dwight Way and Telegraph, where I am standing. Africa tried to continue driving and crashed into a plate glass window of a Mexican restaurant one block further north. According to police Africa began shooting and police unleashed a fusillade of bullets. When the shooting stopped, Africa was dead and the 19 year old female passenger with him was wounded .

(Police spokesman) Police followed accepted procedure. Africa did not follow orders. He shot at our officers.

Ra turned off the TV. He ran his fingers through his afro. "Fuck those police!" He said. "We gotta' do something."

"Like what? Bomb the police?" asked moonshadow.

Ra looked at her. "Why the hell not?"

"No man. I'm just thinkin' about what we can do. Maybe a car or two."

"We could hit the lot where they keep their cruis-ers," suggested Red Dog. "That could be done with fire and no explosives."

Fuckin' cops. Rosie couldn't believe how trigger happy they could be. Even though she was on the same side as they were in this battle against the drug-gies and political wackos, she was truly beginning to understand how people who lived on the edges of the law could end up hating the police. That Rolling Stones song her brother always played on his guitar came to mind—something about every cop a criminal and all the sinners saints.... These guys would hold a serious discussion about a response sometime soon. She knew Ra and the other hardcore NPLFers wouldn't allow the killing of Africa to go unanswered. Not only was it on their turf, but some of the women were good friends of Africa and probably had slept with him at some time or the other. It was up to her to try and stop them. If that didn't work, she needed to at least get them to do something that wouldn't hurt anyone.

"There's no need, guys" broke in Rosie. "To do anything right now. It's too early. See if the city does anything to the cops before we go crazy on 'em. This is Berkeley, you know. Lots of people don't like cops shooting people around here."

moonshadow remembered the first time she met Thomas. She had just pulled into Berkeley from the Dead tour. Ben was gone. Her plan was to go to Merritt College for a couple years and then get into UC Berkeley. It was her third day in town. She had just found a place to live on Dwight Way near the hospital. She was wearing her angel dress—a white filmy thing that made her feel ethereal when she wore it. The dress flowed like a breeze. She always wore a chemise and underwear under it so she didn't expose anything she didn't want exposed. Thomas saw her walking down Telegraph. He was playing a Bob Marley song on his guitar and his dreads were only a few inches long then. She sat down next to him and sang. He smiled. After the song was through they went to Peoples Park and smoked some weed. He was so mellow and soft-spoken. That evening she slept with him at his apartment near San Pablo. She got a job working at a record store a week later and they started seeing each other a lot. The place on Dwight didn't last. Eventually, she ended up at the NPLF house. Then he moved on to another woman. She wasn't jealous or anything but she did miss his soft voice and smile. And now he was dead.

She felt she had to do something. Vengeance wasn't really her thing but this group of people she was hanging out with thought it was the appropriate thing. She had to think about it. She put on her sneakers and left the house. Whenever she needed to think she liked to go to the pier. The walk would do her good. She needed to get outside.

Cat's place. Peter sat on the cushion and watched the news about the cops killing Thomas. Cat came out of the kitchen.

"He was living too fast," she said. "The cops were going to put him down. They didn't like him with all those young white girls." She handed the pack of Pall Malls to Peter. He lit one. Cat went back into the kitchen. He smelt the incense burning. Might as well hang out.

"You wanna' get high?" he asked. He lit the joint in his hand and brought it into the kitchen. Cat took a hit or two and handed it back. Looking outside, Peter noticed it had started raining.

Cat had always been good to Peter. When he first met her on Telegraph, Lucy was at work. Things hadn't been going very well between the two of them. Lucy had just told him that she wanted to live what she called a normal life--a job, partying, and maybe a kid or two, with or without Peter. Peter, meanwhile, was caught up in the streets. Dealing a little here and there, hanging out and meeting the characters that made up the scene around Telegraph and the Haight. Politics had snared his interest again, too. He loved Lucy but couldn't be the person she wanted. Cat was reading tarot when they met. She had grabbed Peter when he walked by her table at the corner of Durant and Telegraph.

"Sit down and I"l give you a reading." Cat pointed toward the folding chair opposite her place at the table. Peter sat down. The only thing he really remembered from the reading was that the Emperor was right side up. That meant something big according to the method Cat was using. They hung out more and more. Never sleeping with each other but enjoying each other's company. Her place was a clearinghouse for all kinds of folks. Hog Farmers, acid dealers, hustlers, street saviors and lost little girls. They came and they went and some of them came back again.

A Week Later

Peter sat in a cell in the Berkeley jail. His memory was replaying itself. After arriving at the station, the cops told him he had been present when a bag of marijuana was sold to a woman officer posing as a college student. According to California law, this made him as liable as the person who actually sold the weed. So much for illegal search and seizure and the Bill of Rights. After carefully recalling his past couple of weeks, he finally recalled the instance. He was turning it over and over, hoping to find some flaw in police procedure which would help him out of this mess. His cellmate threw up in the corner, apparently sick from alcohol. He hoped to hell that he could get out of this one.

Jail. Folks have written about it since before Daniel's time with the lions. Jesus spent some time there and so did Barrabas. Emma Goldman and Huey Newton. The so-called witches of Salem and Joanne Little. Thousands of poor men and women and even a few of the rich and powerful. The place where the keepers keep the kept. Breakfast before dawn. That sadistic cop who beats the shit out of prisoners in the holding cell. The junkies trading their breakfast away for a cigarette since they're too sick to eat anyhow. The big mean mothers looking at the skinny boy's ass. The skinny boy acting crazy like he's a homicidal maniac. The jailhouse convert who discovered the straight and narrow a bit too late.

Peter spent the night. The next morning the jailer opened the gate. Peter walked to the front of the block. Cat had raised his bail. He was out until his court date. It was while Peter lay in jail trying to sleep that a notion hit him. Not a revelation, but a notion. Had what began as a rejection of middle American life as a consumer become a life similar to that of a mere renegade? Now his choices were being made by men and women who embraced the laws that maintained and protected that way. What began as an attempt to be free had become a classic exercise of staying a step ahead of the law. He found the thought depressingly real.

Later, when he appeared in court on the charges, the judge who sentenced him could hardly wait to get out of his robes. He gave Peter a year's probation.

July 1979

Ra sat in the back of the bar sipping on a double screwdriver. He watched the bartender wash glasses and shoot the shit with some brother about the 49ers. They weren't but three or four miles from Candlestick. Pretty close to OJ's old stomping grounds. There were two other people in the bar this early afternoon. A man and a woman slowly getting drunk. Laughing and talking. Occasionally kissing on each other. This was one of the three bars he met up with his so-called handler—a plainclothes detective from California CBI whom he called Stevens. Not a bad guy. A brother. Ra had been working with him ever since he moved out of LA. Got too hot for him down there after the SLA shit. DeFreeze and him had both been working for the cops since before the Panther-US Slaves shootout. DeFreeze got the good gig when they set him up with those sucker white kids from Berkeley. Got himself tons of white tail and had them white folks doing whatever he asked. Even that rich bitch Hearst. The one who snitched 'em all out after getting most of 'em killed. She sang after she got caught with that Asian chick in San Francisco a year or so later. Meanwhile Ra was settin' up angel dust and smack dealers in Compton. Until he got busted with that coke. The charges were dropped. Word got out he knew too many cops and CBI sent him north. Time for another screwdriver. The bartender mixed him up another.

Stevens walked into the bar. He saw Ra immediately. Asked the bartender for a shot of JD and headed back to Ra's table. They shook hands.

"Hey, bro.'" said Stevens. He ran his hands over his shaved head. "Been here long?"

"Long enough to finish a drink." Ra watched as three men came into the bar. Young punks getting off work. They sat at the bar.

"Let me get one down and we'll talk."

The bartender brought Stevens' shot and Ra's screwdriver. Stevens paid. He tossed the shot back and relaxed a little in the booth. Ra took a sip. He cracked his knuckles.

"Any new shit on the kids in Berkeley?" asked Stevens. Ra's primary role was to keep an eye on the NPLF and also to provoke them into doing something that would put them away.

"They talkin' lots about that rasta dealer got shot by the BPD."

"Yeah?"

"Talkin' about how they got to respond," continued Ra. He wasn't in any hurry to put the kids away. Not until he got into Rosie's pants. Plus, this gig was a lot easier than infiltratin' Oakland drug gangs. And he knew that was next once these kids were busted.

"Any word on what they plannin'?" Stevens didn't really trust this guy. Ra was a snitch who had been protected ever since he helped take down the Panthers in LA back in '66 and '67. That and some big bust of some LA cops for runnin' some kind of prostitution gig gave him a permanent gig as a snitch. A snitch is a snitch. He'd rat on anyone to save his ass. Sell out his grandma.

"Nothin' serious. I'll call if they get serious." Ra drained his drink. Stevens bought him another one and tossed back another shot. They talked about football for a few minutes. Stevens left a few hundred on the table for Ra and left. Ra bought another drink. The bar was dark. Now a dozen patrons sat quietly drinking. Curtis on the tape player behind the bar. Blacker than blue.

August 1979

moonshadow was taking Peter to the Mabuhay Gardens. They were on the BART. The band Flipper was headlining. Lots of alcohol. People looking at him funny 'cause of his long hair. Kind of stupid how punks and freaks were supposed to hate each other. Neither had much use for the mainstream bullshit. moonshadow knew a lot of the people here. She looked fuckin' good in black. Huiliang was outside the bar talking politics with punkers, many who considered themselves anarchists.

The first band started up. Peter hung in the back of the bar. moonshadow jumped right in to the crowd. Twenty minutes later the first group was done. Another forty minutes before Flipper. moonshadow went to the back and sat with Peter. He was drinking and talking with Huiliang about the Sandinista victory. The RCP disagreed with the Sandinistas but supported them in their defeat of Somoza. Who didn't besides the right wing? moonshadow took his hands and led him outside. The air smelled like the ocean. Huiliang went back to selling her papers to the punk rockers.

October 1979

In Berkeley the day labor building was off San Pablo. It opened at 7:00 AM. The first people there usually got the jobs. Peter went there in the morning to keep his name on the list. Occasionally he hired on with someone. Most of the work involved either gardening or labor, but occasionally one would actually demand a little skill. When he first got to Berkeley, Peter had worked for an older Sioux woman who needed some gardening. Sixty years old and very beautiful. Long black hair and slender build. For lunch she'd invite him into her fancy house in the Oakland hills and fix a sandwich and a gin and tonic. While they ate and drank she told him stories about her husbands. The last one was a wealthy Spaniard who left his money to her. He died of a heart attack screwing his secretary, like Nelson Rockefeller. Her current husband was away, she said. After a week of lunches she asked Peter to fuck her. Peter asked for another drink. The next time he went to work there, her husband was there with a pistol. She came out the door behind him and told Peter he could stay. He didn't.

About the only other day labor job that stuck in Peter's mind was one which came up every year right before Christmas. Porgy and Peter had been hired three years in a row. It involved sorting trash from recyclables at the Berkeley city dump. The employer was a company which did surveys for municipal waste operations that were supposed to help the interested cities in determining whether or not they should build a waste incinerator. Of course, the ecological implications of the atmospheric waste generated by the burning of the garbage was not part of the quotient. The crew waited for the garbage trucks to come in and dump their loads. Then they would don gloves and pick through the trash, tossing recyclable materials in one pile and garbage in the other. The boss would weigh the stuff.

The reason Peter remembered the job was because of a comment made by Porgy the first year he worked it. It was before the boss man had shown up for the day. The workers were sitting around in the dump drinking coffee, smoking cigarettes and throwing rocks at the gulls who feasted off the waste of Berkeley's humans. The conversation was primarily about the upcoming holiday and poverty. Peter started to say something. Porgy put his stocking cap over his afro, looked right at Peter and the other white guys on the crew and said: "Hell, you guys could cut off your hair and beards and get right back into the white man's system. I can't wash my skin off. Nothing against you guys, but it's the fuckin' truth."

November 1979

The occupation of People's Park was over. The support it had garnered from the community had dissipated. The party had been great. Now nobody but street people occupied it. On Thanksgiving the cops came in and hauled everyone who didn't leave away. The space had transformed though. No asphalt was left except along the borders to the street. There it was piled up like a barricade. Several trees had been planted and a stage constructed. The University-- which owned the property-- would leave it alone for a little while. Peter, Porgy and Roger had been present at the final stand. Which really wasn't much of a stand at all. The cops came in with two vans and a cruiser. They locked up half of the people there on old warrants and left the rest of them standing around. The rain came down.

December 1979

It was late. After midnight. Peter's shack. Roger and Peter were smoking weed and eating Chinese takeout with moonshadow. It had been a week since Roger had last seen Rosie. She made it clear that she would get in touch with him not the other way around. The trip back east had been delayed. Woody was up in Washington trying to convince an old girlfriend to get back with him. Roger didn't know enough about the circumstances to wager on Woody's success. His beeper beeped. It was Rosie. He took another bite of the veggie lo mein and left. There was a pay phone by the liquor store a block away.

Two Nights Later

Another late night in December. Porgy, Rhiannon and Turtle from the NPLF house were on their bicycles. They had spent weeks preparing for this action. Once they knew they had to do something, they convinced the rest of the cadre to let them carry it out. The molotovs were just right. Their surveillance had told them that 3 AM was the best time to hit the lot. Most of the cops on duty would be eating at the Denny's in Emeryville. They rode their bikes silently up the street behind the jail. Dressed in black, the three stopped, quickly lit the gasoline soaked rags and tossed the molotovs. Two of them hit cars and the third exploded near the building. The fire spread and two cars caught. The bicyclists left quickly, riding north towards Live Oak Park. Once they reached the park, they took a left and headed towards San Pablo Avenue. There they left their bikes at a bike stand in front of the Ashkenaz and walked west a couple blocks. From there they snaked their way up to Albany. They then knocked on the door of a friend who let them in for the night.

moonshadow and Ra were at the NPLF house with Rosie, Red Dog and the two other women of the cell, Tian and Lynelle. They remained awake until a call came through. The caller told them to listen to KPFA in the morning. moonshadow went to bed. She was nearly asleep when she felt Ra's presence in the room. She ignored him, figuring that he was just going to crash on the other mattress. Instead, he lay down next to her and began to grab her breasts. She pulled away.

"Go away, Ra," she said. She rolled away from him.

"Oh come on, you want some lovin'." He grabbed her hips and pulled her towards him.

"I got a lover, Ra. Leave me alone." She pushed his hands off and moved away from him.

"Oh, now we getting all monogamy on me." She heard him taking off his pants. She sat up.

"Ra," she said louder than before. "I'm not interested. Leave me alone."

He ignored her and grabbed her breasts again. moonshadow pushed him away and stood up. Ra grabbed at her and slapped her face. She jumped up from the mattress and pulled on a shirt and pants. She went quickly to the door and ran out. She couldn't decide whether to stay in the house or go to Peter's. She looked in on Rosie who was asleep. Before she closed the door she locked it to protect her from Ra and slipped out of the house.

6:30 AM. moonshadow was awake. She turned on the radio to KPFA. News. A Soviet invasion of Afghanistan underway. Two Berkeley police cars burned overnight. "A note sent to this station from the New People's Liberation Front claimed responsibility. The note stated that the attacks were in response for the police murder of Thomas Africa several weeks ago. Police spokesperson Jeannette Michaels told reporters police are hunting down the suspects now."

moonshadow woke up Peter. Her joining him overnight had been a pleasant surprise. He opened his eyes. He pulled her towards him and kissed her breasts.

"Peter, we gotta' go. Two cop cars were burned last night. They're gonna' be looking."

"Huh." Peter sat up. "You weren't involved. You don't have to worry. Remember, you opposed the action." He stroked her hair.

"The pigs don't know that." moonshadow was suddenly scared. She hadn't felt like this since the time she was busted in Oakland for acid at a Grateful Dead show. She shook for a fuckin' hour then. The cops laughed the whole time they were questioning her.

She told Peter that Ra had tried to fuck her again. "I don't really want to stay there while he's around. If I leave, though, they'll think I'm a cop."

"Let's go to Cat's."

They got dressed, locked the place up and walked to Cat's, taking a circuitous route through Berkeley and Oakland. Cat was still asleep when they arrived. Peter had a key and let them in. Cat heard them and said hello. Peter gave her a quick rundown of the situation. They climbed into the loft and went back to sleep.

An hour later, Roger knocked on Cat's door. She unlocked it and let him in. A huge smile on his face. He reached into his backpack and pulled out a dozen eggs, some cheese, butter and a pound of coffee. He looked in the loft, saw Peter and moonshadow and nodded hello. Despite his romance with Rosie, Roger had no idea she or moonshadow were involved with the NPLF. Nor had he heard the news of the fire-bombing. Cat knew enough to keep quiet. After all, she was the holder of many secrets--her own and those of many others. It was a role she was made for.

"You bring gifts!" said Cat. She took the food and set it next to the stove. "We eat! Peter, come help me cook this up." She began to move pans around on the stove while Peter recovered some utensils from the sink and washed them. Roger thumbed through the albums Cat had collected from various guests and friends. He chose Moby Grape's first. moonshadow put some clothes on and joined him. Cat served the breakfast she and Peter had cooked. The four of them spent the day there, drinking malt liquor, smoking weed, and conversing with whoever stopped by. Southwester showed up in the early afternoon. He and Cat had a thing going that went hot and cold like water coming from a broken tap. More people continued to show up. By evening the party was pretty damned boisterous. Around seven that night Peter left with Southwester to buy another case of beer.

When they had settled in back at the place, Cat put on a record and cooked up some burritos. Folks continued to come and go, bringing more beer with them. Around ten o'clock there was a loud knock on the door. Peter opened it to find a policeman standing on the porch with his nightstick in his hand.

"Turn down the music," he commanded.

"Sure, just a minute," Peter replied.

"Do it now!"

"Wait a goddam minute and I will!" yelled Peter. Just then Cat was in the doorway, a beer in her hand and her long hair across her face.

"What's his fuckin' problem, Peter? Is this pig botherin' you?" she began. Peter turned his attention to Cat and asked her to be mellow so the cop wouldn't come in the house.

She continued yelling, this time at the officer. "Fuck you man. We'll play our music as loud as we want!" Meanwhile Southwester had turned the volume on the stereo down to a much softer level.

The cop looked at Cat, thought about saying something but instead turned around and left. As soon as he did Peter closed the door. He sat back down on the couch, hoping the cop would not come back that evening. Cat had other ideas. She turned the music up even louder than before. Within minutes the cop was back at the door pounding on it with his nightstick. He seemed to be looking for a fight. Cat opened the door once again and then attempted to slam the door in his face. He reacted by applying a karate-like kick to where the door was connected to the frame and tore the door completely from its hinges. After taking note of the destruction, the cop backed away and began talking on his radio. Southwester pulled Cat away from the door, hoping that would be the end of what could become a very ugly scene which would probably end in the arrest of everyone.

The apartment had a rear door. Peter headed there. He hoped to approach the officer outside to try and talk with him quietly in the hopes that he would go way if Peter promised to turn off the music for the night. By the time Peter reached the front of the building there were six cops standing in front of the apartment with their nightsticks out. The door to the apartment was open. As soon as Peter appeared near them one of the policemen attacked. Within minutes he was on the ground with three officers on him. One was twisting his arms around and the other two were pushing his face into the concrete of the sidewalk. He was thrown into the cruiser belonging to the cop who began the whole episode. When they got to the jail he put Peter in a holding cell and began to beat him. If it weren't for the jailer arriving, Peter would have been beaten unconscious. The jailer told the arresting officer to go file his report. He kicked Peter once more. While the jailer wrote down his information Peter asked why the previous cop was so sadistic. She answered that he had been a military man in the South Vietnamese Army whose job was to extract information from the Viet Cong.

March 1980

The firebombing was more than two months in the past. Cops were making things a little warm. Unmarked cars across the street from the house. Turtle and Rhiannon pulled over and were warned they should leave town. Still no arrests, though. Rosie and Ra hadn't been at the house for a week. No one had seen them since they left for Marin to buy some acid. The group had finally pulled together the few thousand dollars they needed for the drugs. moonshadow had been splitting her time between Peter's place and the NPLF house. She told Peter she didn't want them to think she was flaking out on them. Ever since she refused to go along with the car burning action, some of them had been treating her like she was a narc. The discussions since then had centered quite often on the fear that the group was infiltrated. Ra kept throwing the suspicion towards moonshadow and Rosie—the two women in the group that hadn't slept with him. moonshadow had taken advantage of Ra's absence to mend fences in the group. That required her spending time with them, doing self-criticism stuff, and just hanging out. Part of her wanted out but she didn't think the time was right to bring that up. The cops breathing down their necks over the firebombing and now two members missing. Paranoia reigned.

Morning muster Berkeley Police. Two detectives from Marin at the front. The Berkeley Chief introduced them. He began.

"We have information on an apparent homicide that occurred last week. The body of a caucasian female was found about a mile from the Richmond Bridge on the Marin side. From forensics it appears that she was murdered beforehand and her corpse was left. She was last seen in the company of a black male. This identification was made by a gas station attendant in San Rafael the night the victim went missing. Furthermore, hairs appearing to be from a black male were found on her clothes. There was sexual activity but no sign of struggle. However, barbiturates were found in her bloodstream. Victim was an undercover agent for the DEA, and CBI. She was investigating an LSD distribution network based in San Rafael. Some of you may also know that she was an infiltrator of the NPLF group here in Berkeley. Although we have no clear leads and do not know if the murder was random or targeted, the investigation will begin within these two groups. There are two black men in these groups that we know of. One is named Porgy Johnson

The other, who goes by the name Ra, works for the police and has been working for the police since '64, beginning in LA on drug distribution, and then Black Panther jobs. He also helped us recruit Donald De Freeze who you may remember was instrumental in the SLA operation. This informant's primary work is with the NPLF but he supposedly does have some knowledge of the LSD group, as well. Once we make contact with him, we will see if he can get into their good graces. A press conference is scheduled for this afternoon. No mention will be made of the victim's connections to the police, for obvious reasons. In addition, it will be suggested that the male informant is a suspect and no mention will be made of his connection to law enforcement. That's all. Get your assignments from the Sergeant."

That Afternoon

Peter was in a Berkeley cop car. He wasn't surprised. The fact that Rosie and Ra were apparently missing was common knowledge on the street. His relationship with moonshadow had to give the cops cause for suspicion. Their excuse was an open container. He was walking to his place from the BART station when they grabbed him. While in the car, a radio transmission had come over from dispatch. The dispatch was about Porgy. Some kind of APB. After the dispatch ended, the two cops in the car began talking about the murder of a female named McNamara in Marin. The way they talked it was clear they thought Porgy was the killer. At the station they threw Peter into a holding cell. Later, they took him to a room and asked him if he knew anything about either the firebombings or Rosie's death. Peter said it was the first he had heard about Rosie being dead. They asked if he knew her. He told them he did, but not well. They asked him about Porgy's relationship to her. Peter said nothing. They asked about the firebombings. While he sat in the cell, he wondered why they had not asked about Ra. In an unexpected insight, Peter began to wonder if Ra might be working for the cops. As far as Peter knew, Ra was still walking around trying to fuck hippie chicks.

The next morning he got out. Walking away from the jail he saw Ra going in the front door of the courthouse with a couple plainclothes cops. He wasn't handcuffed. Peter hid his face and walked away quickly. He jumped on a bus going down Martin Luther King Way.

moonshadow was at his place when he arrived. She pulled Peter towards her and kissed him. Peter held back. His sighting of Ra and the questions he'd been asked made him nervous.

"We gotta' get out of here," said Peter. "The cops must be watching us. I'll tell you more once we're gone. I know I thought you were overreacting, but now I think you might be right."

"Let me just do this," said moonshadow. She knelt down and unzipped Peter's jeans. Peter gave in. He reached down and pulled off her t-shirt.

Their escapade complete, moonshadow zipped up his pants and pulled her t-shirt on. She ran her fingers through his hair. Peter found his backpack and threw some clothes and other items in. moonshadow followed suit.

"We'll go to Rodeo," said Peter. "Rosie's dead. The cops let it slip while they asked me about her and the firebombings. The cops are probably looking for you. I heard them say they were looking for Porgy. It sounded like they think he killed Rosie. I have a friend named Hawk in Rodeo that I don't think the cops know about. Hopefully they won't follow us." He continued to pack. He was glad he didn't have any dope at the house. It made getting out of there a lot easier. moonshadow tightened the straps on her backpack and headed toward the door. A cop car was in front of the house next door. Two cops sat in it.

"Wait," said Peter. "We'll climb out the back window and go through the churchyard behind us. We'll go to Cat's first."

moonshadow climbed out the window. Peter followed. A bus was approaching the stop in front of the church behind Peter's house. They ran to the stop and boarded the bus. It took them down Telegraph to Oakland. They got off near Cat's, stopped to buy some wine and headed to her apartment. They could leave the next morning for Rodeo. Cat had a car and would drive them.

Peter was in Cat's main room considering everything he had heard and seen while in custody and immediately after. Cat was cooking dinner. She and moonshadow were talking and laughing in the kitchen. Peter rolled a joint and brought it in to the two of them. After a couple tokes, he looked at Cat.

"When I left the jail I saw Ra going in the front with a couple cops. He wasn't handcuffed or nothin'" said Peter.

"And you said they're looking for Porgy?" asked Cat.

"Yeah, that's mostly who they were asking me about. I told them I didn't know where he was, of course."

Cat thought quietly, sucking in the reefer smoke. "Ra must be working for 'em or something," she said. "In the news conference the cops said they were looking for two black guys. You would think Ra had to be one of them. But why wouldn't they be looking for him, too? Unless he's a pig." She looked pissed off. She jumped to a conclusion. She brushed some ash from her shirt. "I never did trust that fucker. Didn't you all say her and Ra went over to Marin together?"

"Yeah," said moonshadow. "Roger offered but Rosie didn't want him to know anything about her NPLF work. He never came to the house. They always met somewhere and stayed at a hotel. She insisted that Ra drive her to Fats."

One more glass of wine. Dinner followed.

Early the next morning. Porgy was nervous. Word on the street was that the cops wanted him. Wanted him for questioning, but he had a feeling it was more than that. Only thing he could figure was that it had to do with the firebombings of the cruisers. Shit. They'd beat on him if they caught him, he knew that. Always did before. He sat in his camp near the marina. Hadn't been back to the house for three days. He had used this camp for years as a hideout. It was well hidden.

He had enough food and smoke to hide for a few days as long as no one saw him. Thing was, up until now he thought they had fingered someone else for burning the cruisers since they never came after him and the sisters at the house. Maybe someone in the house talked too much and the cops got the word. Maybe the cops just wanted to pin the action on someone so they could move on. Either way his life was getting pretty fuckin' uncomfortable.

He heard someone coming. Crouching down in the marsh grasses he watched Red Dog from the house go by. Red Dog looked around but didn't see Porgy. He was carrying a six-pack and a newspaper.

"Porgy!" Red Dog whispered. "Where you at?" Porgy shifted his weight and Red Dog looked toward the sound of the moving grass. He saw Porgy and walked into the grass. Porgy nodded toward Red Dog and Red Dog sat down on a milk crate. He gave Porgy a beer and the paper.

"Check it out," said Red Dog, pointing at a headline. "They found Rosie's body. She was killed over a week ago."

Porgy took the paper and read the article. Essentially a police report. Said she was found near the Richmond Bridge on the Marin side. Hairs found on her clothing and body appeared to be from a black male. Sexually assaulted although no evidence of resistance. Drugs found in her system--barbiturates and narcotics. That was weird. Rosie hated downers and narcotics. Said the cops were looking for two black men whom she affiliated with for questioning. Porgy just knew he was one of them. Ra must be the other.

"There's some other stuff they didn't write in that article," began Red Dog. "Like Rosie was a narc. She must have been trying to bust those acid dealers in Marin."

"Does moonshadow know this?" asked Porgy. "She's the one brought her over there."

"I doubt it. I just found out this morning from an undercover cop who was shaking me down on Telegraph. I made some remark. He laughed and let it slip that we were all gonna' go down because we were too stupid to figure out that we had had a narc in our midst."

"Is Ra around?"

"Nobody knows where the hell he is."

Porgy knew for sure now that the cops would be looking for him. Even worse, now the charge would probably be murder. Of a cop. He had to do something. Go deeper underground. Red Dog opened another beer and took a drink.

"So, what we gonna' do?" asked Porgy. "I mean, is anyone at the house?"

"Nah. Most of the women are disappearing into the woodwork. Hiding out up north in Humboldt somewheres. I'm taking a bus out of here and going to Oregon this afternoon. moonshadow went somewhere with her boyfriend. I'm supposed to help you get the hell out of Dodge. I can get you a ride to St. Louis that leaves this afternoon if you want. I know you got people there."

Porgy thought about it. He hadn't been home for five years. There wasn't much there for him if he did go. But he wasn't ready to stay here and get busted. What the fuck, he would take the ride. He could always get out anywhere along the way. They would have to activate their contact system. Tuesdays between 7 and 8 PM everyone call a certain number and get any instructions and news. Memorize the mailing address at the private mailbox service on Shattuck.

"Yeah. I'll take that ride," said Porgy. It was the best option.

"Here's the numbers for Tuesdays and the mailing address." Red Dog gave him a piece of paper. Porgy memorized the numbers and ate the scrap of paper it was printed on. A little secret agent shit. The numbers were pay phones. Red Dog told him that Peter would be the guy relaying the information. The phones rotated every other week. Peter volunteered because moonshadow had asked him too. Even though he had his misgivings about getting involved, he knew he had to do something. Since he had virtually nothing to do with the NPLF and his connection with the San Rafael drug operation was minimal he seemed like the best choice. He had introduced Roger to Fats, but that was about it. He partied with the people there but was not in business with them. Even the quarter-gram of LSD

Roger had fronted him he had returned to Roger.

"The car will be here at noon. It's a green Datsun 210. They'll drive up by the road over there...." Red Dog pointed toward the road that went into the Marina. "and wait for you for five minutes. Then they'll leave. Be ready. If I were you I would destroy this camp you got here as much as you can."

Porgy looked around. A little housekeeping should do the trick. Bury some of the trash and burn a couple pieces of paper that might give a hint as to his person.

Red Dog gave Porgy a hug. "Take it easy, bro. Keep the faith and all that stuff."

"You too, man." Red Dog finished his beer and walked away from Porgy's camp. Porgy watched him go.

Peter and moonshadow were in Rodeo. Hawk was out of town but Peter had a key to the house. It was a small rambler type place set back from a small single lane road. It sat on a couple acres. There were a couple old cars in the yard setting on blocks and an old washing machine. Two dogs watched the place. They knew Peter well and seemed to like moonshadow. She played with the dogs while Peter cooked up a small meal from some canned goods he found in the cupboard. Roger had called Cat's right before Peter left her house. Said he was coming over. Peter didn't tell him they were going to Hawk's, but asked Cat to let him know if he asked.

It was dusk. moonshadow and Peter were eating.

The dogs were on the porch relaxing after sharing some of the canned stew Peter had warmed up. moonshadow took the dishes to the sink. She came back and sat on Peter's lap. He felt his pants tighten. They began kissing as moonshadow wrapped her legs around his back. Just then the dogs began to bark. moonshadow unwrapped her legs and Peter got up. He went over to the window and recognized Roger's truck. He pulled into the long driveway and turned off his lights and engine, letting the truck roll to a stop. Inside the truck, Roger pulled up the emergency brake and got out. He walked quickly and quietly to the house. moonshadow let him in.

"Hey." Roger nodded at Peter and hugged moon-shadow. He looked a bit out of sorts.

"Have a seat, man." Peter gestured to the couch. Roger sat down. His hair was sweaty and his shirt was muddy.

"You all must know..." he said.

"Yeah," said Peter.

"I can't believe she's fuckin' dead. I hardly knew her. What, I hung out with her for a couple months. We had somethin' though."

"I hate to tell you this, bro...." began Peter. "But she was a narc."

Roger looked up. He hadn't known. "Bullshit!"

"No man. I wouldn't bullshit you about something like that. Nobody knew until this morning. A friend of moonshadow's found out from a Berkeley pig when he got shook down."

Roger looked a little stunned. How could he have not sensed that? Shit. This connection might bring the entire heat down on Fats. Fuck. He had to let them know. No time for sorrow. Not even time for a bong hit.

"I gotta' go. Let me call Fats and tell him I'm coming." Roger left Peter and moonshadow as quickly as he had come.

Peter got up the next morning and turned on the radio. A news item mentioned a ranch being burnt down in Marin. Nobody was hurt and some horses were running free. It sounded like Fats' place. The reporter mentioned that the ranch had once belonged to the members of Quicksilver Messenger Service. It had to be Fats' place. He wondered if Roger had been with Fats and who actually set the fire. He was betting that Fats was already in Hawaii making himself scarce. Fats had said he knew some Brotherhood people there.

The NPLF house on San Pablo the same morning. Fifteen cops in SWAT uniforms stood around waiting for their orders. Two cops in regular uniforms knocked on the door. Sixty or so neighborhood residents stood on the other side of the street watching the cops. After about five minutes the SWAT team moved into place. Two of the biggest members went up the steps and kicked the door down. The bottom half of the door caved in but the deadbolts prevented the entire door from being ripped off the jamb. Another cop took a sledgehammer and broke up the rest of the door. The cops went in with their weapons drawn. Sidearms, shotguns, semiautomatics. They shouted Police! Police! While inside they tore up the house as much as possible. Nobody home. Most of the SWAT team left after an hour. The rest remained to guard the shattered and open house.

Peter and moonshadow watched the raid on the news that evening while they ate more canned goods and shared them with the dogs. Hawk was coming back into town in the next day or two. Peter contrived a plan while he laid there with moonshadow in his arms. He knew she was going to be wanted and the cops would be looking for her. He wasn't so sure about his status. He didn't want any surprises, though. It would probably be best for Hawk if the cops never traced the two of them back to Hawk's place.

"I should get a lawyer." It was as if moonshadow had read his thoughts. "Maybe they could engineer a way for me to turn myself in." She sat up quickly and began to pace around in the small room. The dogs followed her, wagging their tails as if they expected her to play with them. Peter listened.

"You know they're going to try and round us all up as material witnesses or something," said moonshadow. "I could probably get the jump on them if a

92

lawyer arranged for me to meet them. The only thing is I don't know how the others would take it. I don't want them to think I'm narcing them out."

"I don't think they would," said Peter. "But you gotta' watch out for them cops. They can trick you."

"It's better if I have a lawyer then. He or she could tell me when to shut up so I don't get anyone into trouble."

Peter nodded. That made sense. "You know anyone?" he asked.

"Ben had some dude he used to go to when he needed help with money and getting his buddies out of jail," remembered moonshadow. "John Meredith was his name I think. He did some political stuff, too. I think with the Black Panthers. I'm sure we could find his number in the phone book." She began to look for a phone book in Hawk's house. After opening and closing several drawers, she found one in a closet. She paged through it.

"Yeah, here he is." she smiled. "John Meredith."

"I'll call him first thing tomorrow," promised Peter. He pulled moonshadow to him and they began kissing. He wanted this lovemaking to last all night. moonshadow might be in jail tomorrow. He wondered again if he should worry about himself.

After Peter fell asleep moonshadow sat in the house. She was thinking about Rosie's death. She could hear Ra's smooth words turn to pleading and then anger. She saw his caresses turn to forceful grips and slaps. She heard

Rosie's requests, felt her struggle and then knew she had given in, allowing Ra to have his way. She wondered if Rosie had taken the downers at Fats or if Ra had slipped them into a drink beforehand. What she didn't see was the fatal attack in the Marin night. Probably some dirt road between San Rafael and San Quentin. The location didn't matter really. It was the fear that was the true place things like that happened.

Yet, she was a narc. It pulled moonshadow and everyone else who knew her in two directions. Yeah, she was a narc, but had her share of contradictions. Conflicted was what Peter said. It seemed like Rosie agreed with the NPLF at times. moonshadow didn't have much sympathy for her and the role she had chosen. But she didn't think she deserved to die.

The lawyer's office was in the Bayview District of San Francisco. Nice little house not too far from the ocean. Peter sat in the waiting room while moonshadow talked with Meredith in his office. He read the *Chronicle*. There was a story about the NPLF. How they were suspected of the firebombing of Berkeley police cars after the Berkeley cops killed Thomas Africa. How they were connected to the SLA via some political connections forged in People's Park during the 1972 riots there. Peter thought the latter element was really grasping at straws. There was also a mention of the connection between the NPLF and Fats' operation. That connection, said the story, was uncovered by the deceased, who was an undercover police-woman. In other words, Rosie was the connection between the two groups. As far as Peter knew, this was the first public acknowledgment that Rosie was a narc. The cops must be trying a new tactic. When someone killed a cop, that usually got the sympathy of a certain element of the public. The story said they were looking for Porgy. In fact they mentioned him by name. It also stated that several others were wanted as material witnesses. moonshadow had called that one. Nothing about Ra.

Early April 1980

Porgy got out of the car. He was in Kansas City, Missouri. He had friends here. It was time to leave his ride. No St. Louis for him. The ride had been uneventful so far, but the driver had seen a news item on the TV in the last motel they stayed at that mentioned Porgy's name in connection with some NPLF stuff. Both he and Porgy knew it was time to break it off. They figured Porgy would find it easier to disappear in KC. He thanked the driver and began walking toward the black side of town. Tomorrow was Tuesday.

It was Tuesday. moonshadow had turned herself in. The cops were holding her for at least twenty-four hours. The attorney Meredith had accompanied her inside the Berkeley police station. Meredith had put Peter up in a motel near the ocean just south of Golden Gate Park. Peter watched the story on the noon news in his room. Meredith promised to get a hold of Peter once he left the station. He told Peter to stay away and not to raise the cops' suspicions about his connection to the NPLF, even if it was tangential. Of course, Peter hadn't told Meredith about his phone call role. He waited until late afternoon before he left the motel. He caught a couple buses to Berkeley.

It was time for him to wait by the pay phone. It wasn't more than a five minute walk from where he had disembarked from the bus. Ten minutes later he was talking to Red Dog. He told him about moonshadow's decision. Red Dog agreed that it made sense.

"The shit's been on the news a lot down here," said Peter. "But no mention of Ra." He didn't tell Red Dog about Fats' place going up in flames. Red Dog stated that he was doing fine and was laying low. Peter told him he was wanted as a material witness. Then they ended the call.

Next came a very brief call from Rhiannon. She was well hidden in some lesbian communes in the Southwest. Rhiannon was reporting for the others as well. No phones and no television. Peter filled them in quickly on the Bay Area situation and terminated the call.

Next came Porgy. Peter answered on the second ring. He could hear the noise of the Kansas City streets in the background.

"Hey man," began Porgy. "What's up? I'm all right."

Peter wanted to ask him where he was but thought better of it. "They're looking for you, man. Stay low." He brought Porgy up to date and hung up. No one else was supposed to call tonight. Turtle was just gone. Probably back to the Trinity Alps where she hid out every few months. Walking away from the pay phone Peter laughed to himself. How had he become the go-between for this group of revolutionary pretenders? He was reminded of Neil Young's song "Revolution Blues" or some stupid *National Lampoon* skit. Sure, he sort of agreed with the basic elements of their politics, but they had thrown him out of their house. He was friends with Porgy from the street and lovers with moonshadow, but he considered them friends, not just political allies. As for Ra and Rosie--well one of them was a narc and dead and the other one was just a slimy kind of guy who probably killed the narc.

Peter continued on his way to the Ashby BART station. The motel Meredith had put him up in was a quiet place with very little traffic. He was supposed to stay there until moonshadow got out. He would probably move before that. After taking the BART to the Mission, he walked back up to Market and caught a streetcar out to the Rainbow Market. He grabbed some beers and other supplies and walked the remaining distance to the motel.

May 1980

Two weeks later, moonshadow was given three months in prison for an old pot charge the cops had found.. They couldn't connect her to the NPLF crime or Rosie's murder, but refused to let her go unless she pleaded to something. She copped the plea. She hadn't provided them with any incriminating info on the fire-bombings of the cop cars and told them only what she knew about Rosie and Ra's trip to Marin. Her part in setting up the acid deal never came up and as far as the cops knew she had told them everything she knew about it. Peter talked to her before they took her away to Santa Rita. It was hard to watch her leave. If things went well, she would be out in eight weeks.

Peter was still at the motel. Meredith had paid for three weeks and Peter still had a little less than one more week to go. Tuesday calls were still made. Nothing had changed. Porgy was sounding a little ragged from his life on the city streets. The rest of the cadre were doing well in the country.

Peter was watching the evening news at the motel.

The first story had to do with the hostages in Tehran. Peter had to admit that the Iranians that had done this deed sure had a sense of theatre. The great American hero had become a hostage. A bit pathetic. It was hard for all the gringos who saw their masculinity in Washington's wars and imperial domination. Like getting one's balls crushed. The revolution itself was getting kind of murky, though.

The next story began with Porgy's picture covering the screen. Peter turned up the volume.

> *Porgy Freedom Johnson was added to the FBI's Most Wanted list today. He has been charged with the brutal rape and murder of police undercover agent Rosa McNamara. Johnson was charged after new revelations came forward from a police informer who was on the scene prior to McNamara's murder. The informer, whose name the police have not released, had dropped McNamara off at the residence where she was to make an undercover buy of a substantial amount of LSD. According to the informer and police, that was the last anyone saw McNamara alive. Johnson was scheduled to pick McNamara up in downtown San Rafael later that evening after the drug buy was made. She was found dead several days later by the Richmond bridge. Johnson has not been seen since. It is believed he left the state.*

Peter sat up. What fuckin' bullshit. He knew Porgy was not supposed to pick Rosie up after the buy. moonshadow and Roger had told him as much. Porgy was at the house the whole time. Roger wanted to bring her back to the East Bay, but Rosie insisted Ra drive. It was how they had set it up, she said. When Roger was told that he had assumed that Rosie was just practicing a little security. After it came out that Rosie was a narc, Peter began to think that she was protecting Roger. Now he wasn't so sure. Ra was the missing piece in this puzzle. Peter would bet his last dollar that Ra was the informer that had fed the cops this story. That intuitive sense he had that Ra was not only not trustworthy but also dangerous fed his suspicions about the man. He wondered what the hell had happened to Roger.

The third Tuesday. Peter waited at the pay phone. Porgy was the only one of the group who called.

"Peter…."

"What's up, Porgy?" He sensed some alarm in Porgy's voice.

"My cousin told me they got me on the FBI list."

"He's right." Peter waited. He was unsure what to tell Porgy and how much to say on the phone. He didn't think he was being watched but he wasn't certain. He looked around him.

"I got to get out of here." Porgy kept an eye on any unusual movement around the phone booth he was in in Kansas City. He figured he would have to go to Mexico or some other place outside the country.

"Send me a letter to the PO box," instructed Peter. "Give me a phone number and a time. I'll see what I can do to get you out of the country." He hung up the phone and hoped Porgy remembered the PO box number. He knew there would be no phone calls for a couple weeks. It was time to figure out a way to get Porgy gone.

moonshadow had never been in jail before. Her first night was a bit scary but most of the women seemed cool. Her cellmate was another white girl there for heroin and cocaine sales. She was around moonshadow's age and was decidedly hetero, as she made clear to moonshadow the very first night. It was moonshadow's second week now. Somebody had given her a bunch of detective novels to read. Between that and the conversations, time wasn't dragging. It wasn't moving quickly either. Peter visited on Sundays. He couldn't say much about what was going on with the rest of her housemates because of the guards and other surveillance, but it was nice. They talked about splitting from the Bay Area when she got out. She was game. The cops would be watching her every step if she stayed. Might as well go some place new.

Peter was on Haight Street. It was four days after he had spoken with Porgy. He sat at the Pall Mall Tavern drinking a pitcher of beer. There had been so many times he sat there waiting on a connection or just re-laxing. This time was different. The bartender turned up the music. "Can't You Hear Me Knockin'?" by the Stones. Southwester came in and sat next to Peter. He asked for a glass and poured a beer from the pitcher. The two men clinked their glasses.

"Cheers," nodded Southwester. They drained the glasses and poured another.

"Hey, Southwester. Thanks for comin'." Peter grabbed the pitcher and stood up. "Let's get a booth." He asked the bartender to keep the pitchers coming. They moved to a just-vacated booth in the back of the bar. The bar itself was long and narrow like a galley on a ship. There were two rooms. The front room had a bar, some booths and a table. The back room had two pool tables. There was also a door past the bathrooms that opened into an alley. Dealers liked that door as a means of departure.

"So, what's up, Peter?" asked Southwester. "I ain't seen you in a while. That girl been keepin' you busy?"

"She's in jail," Peter said. "Dead Flowers" was the song on the bar stereo.

"Oh, shit. Somethin' to do with that firebombing?" Southwester wasn't sure, but he had heard that moon-shadow was part of the NPLF household.

"Kind of," said Peter. "She turned herself in as a material witness over the murder of that narc--you must have heard about it on the news or somethin'-- and then copped a plea on an old pot charge. She's doin' three months in Santa Rita."

"When she gettin' out?"

"Three or four more weeks unless they fuck with her some more." Peter bummed a cigarette from a woman in the next booth. He had started smoking every once in a while after moonshadow went down.

"What about everyone else?" Southwester asked. "Don't tell me anything you shouldn't."

"That's kind of why I called, man." Peter looked around. There were only three other people in the bar besides Southwester, the bartender and him. He knew all of them at least casually. "I need some ID for Porgy. A passport."

Southwester nodded. "Let's finish the beer and go for a walk."

"What you been doin' anyhow?" asked Peter.

"I been up in Humboldt working." Southwester and a couple of his friends had a few marijuana patches they took care of. It was planting time. Peter considered himself fortunate that Southwester had taken the time to come down to the city. They finished the beer, left the bar and headed west towards Golden Gate Park. After passing through the tunnel at the end of Haight Street they took a right and wandered away from the road that wound through the park. There were some places the two of them favored for making deals and smoking weed. Peter had a passport photograph of Porgy. He handed it to Southwester as they walked.

"When do you need this?" asked Southwester once they had reached one of their spots.

"As soon as possible," answered Peter. "Porgy is on his way to Tucson now from KC. He's going to stay at a friend's place somewhere in town. That's where I'm mailing the thing." A couple walked by the spot where the two men were hiding and talking. They kept going.

"I'll meet you at the Main Library in three days. Look for me in the periodical section." Southwester hugged Peter and left. "Bring four hundred bucks." He headed back towards Haight Street. Peter waited five minutes before he left the hiding place and walked the opposite direction that Southwester had gone.

Two Weeks Later

Porgy waited in the bar as he had been instructed. His wariness enhanced thanks to the increased paranoia he felt from seeing his picture on the post office wall with the rest of the FBI's most wanted, he sipped on a whiskey and water slowly. He wanted to relax but he didn't want to be sloppy or tired. The jukebox played "Freddy's Dead." Porgy sat in a booth far from the door but with a good view of it. Anybody looking for him could see his silhouette in the bar's smoky shadows. Hopefully, that anybody would be the brother who was supposed to give him a ride to Tucson and not some kind of pig looking to bust him.

June 1980

Porgy was in Tucson. The place he was staying belonged to an extremely wealthy couple. There was even an indoor pool. No servants, but a refrigerator in every bedroom. Porgy was given a room near the back of the house that had its own entrance. It's not that he was going anywhere but it could be used for an escape should the need arise. Nothing like that seemed very likely. The place was quiet. The woman who lived there was an artist. The guy a retired journalist. He spoke with the man or woman of the house at least once a day and swam often. The two owners were into drinking wine and smoking a lot of weed. Porgy did drink a bit of wine in the evening, but stayed away from the weed. He needed to keep a clear head. The ride to Tucson was smooth. He had been at this house for three days. No communication from Peter but he expected the passport in the next couple days. Then he was getting a ride to Nogales. From there he would walk across the border and catch a bus on his way to Oaxaca.

Middle of June 1980

His first days in Mexico were a mixture of relief and fear. Of course, the further he got from the border, the better he felt. By the time he made it to Oaxaca, he had one impression. He was alone. According to the passport Peter had sent him, his name was now Esteban Cruz. Porgy often forgot to answer when somebody called him that name. If anything, the nearly naked kids, the smell of sewage and the extremely hot weather and food reminded him of the three years he had spent as a kid in Pakistan. The only black family on the small air base, his parents took him down to the bazaar in Peshawar almost every weekend. His dad thought it important that Porgy know that most people weren't white. The memories he had of that time and place were mostly pleasant except for some of the racist kids he went to school with. Kids who were merely repeating what they heard at home but it still hurt.

He didn't know much Spanish but could order beer and food and find a place to sleep. His plan was to go up to the mountains where some friend of Peter's lived with a couple German women. Then Porgy had to find his own gig. He sat in a Oaxaca cantina drinking beers. Saw two obviously European women and started talking. Talk about luck. They were connected to Peter's friends. They drank until midnight. Porgy found a room and made plans to meet them in the morning for a ride up 175 and then off to the east. Porgy slept well because of the beer.

The next morning he met the two women. The one with the truck drove him up a long winding road to a small ranch with a sprawling adobe house. Must have been six or seven adults who lived there, all German and Austrian. They all spoke Spanish, German and English. Some of them had romances going with some of the locals. There were a few kids that lived there, too. Local kids came and went. The local people were mostly of Mayan ancestry. Very noble people. Porgy learned Spanish in about six months. Did a lot of farming and other work around the place. Took him a while to relax, but he felt safe almost right away.

2007

Peter was finally going to visit Porgy. He had been in town a week but the cops and courts were operating at their usual speed—slower than molasses when it came to helping a prisoner. Anyhow, he had met with Ms. Callahan (or Mariah as she preferred) a couple of times. She was a pretty woman in her early forties. The first day they met she took him to lunch and they had a fairly good time. The child of a black woman and a father who was half Irish and half Japanese. Her parents were both lawyers, quite well off and from Marin County. Consequently, Mariah had grown up around rock musicians, artists, hippies and lawyers. Her regular clients included a couple big time drug dealers, a rock band or two and several non-profits and political organizations of the left wing variety. Peter felt comfortable around her and with her representation of Porgy. He had laid out the basics of his recollections at his second visit in her office. After the meeting, Mariah had asked him to dinner but he declined. He was planning on visiting an old friend who lived in West Oakland.

His friend wasn't home. He hoped he could find Cat somewhere. She seemed to have disappeared from the radar. It seemed that nobody had seen her since the police cleared all of the fortunetellers off of Telegraph Ave. Like the rest of America, Telegraph was being gentrified by and for people who wanted people to pay to be hip. Fortunetellers and street musicians were the first to go in the sweeps conducted by the petit bourgeois city officials and their bully boy cops.

June 1980

Richard Stevens sat in the bar on Jack London Square. Ra was supposed to be showing up soon. He had missed the last meeting. Ra's disappearance didn't look too good to Stevens. Didn't matter what he thought, though. He found it harder to pretend that he liked the guy. Sacramento had told him to keep the snitch on the payroll. In fact, he had a few thousand in an envelope for him right now. He drained his beer and asked for another. The bartender poured him one. The jukebox was playing the Temptations "I Can't Get Next To You." One of Stevens' favorites. He saw Ra come in the door. He shook a couple hands, ordered a drink and headed to where Stevens was sitting. After he sat down, Stevens nodded slightly.

"How you been?" asked Ra.

"I'm asking the questions," said Stevens. He really didn't trust this sonofabitch and was tired of pretending that he did. "Where you been? You missed our last meeting."

"I been in LA. My mama was sick," answered Ra.

He wasn't gonna' give this guy any satisfaction. Their relationship had soured considerably the past couple of months. He was thinking of asking for another handler. Ra had some goods on Stevens, too. He knew all about how he took down hookers and their pimps, getting free pussy and a cut of the take all along 14th Street in East Oakland.

Stevens nodded again. "We got some troubles," he began.

"I figured," answered Ra.

"All them little white kids done left the city after that Rosa McNamara was found dead. We think they might have discovered she was working with us. Do you know anything about it?"

"I tol' you, man. I been in LA." Ra finished his drink. Stevens motioned to the bartender for two more drinks. "The last time I seen Rosie was when I dropped her off in San Rafael for her to make that acid buy from that white boy calls himself Fats."

"He's gone, too," said Stevens.

"I figured. He's been in the business for awhile. I'm betting he's in Mexico or maybe even Nepal by now. What about that brother Porgy?" Ra asked, remembering that Stevens had only mentioned the white kids in NPLF.

"He's gone, too," said Stevens. "The Berkeley boys broke into the house on San Pablo and found nothing but a few newspapers, some dirty laundry and a little bit of pot. Oh yeah, and some big fireworks."

"Did they watch the buses leaving Oakland?" asked Ra.

"If they did, they didn't catch no one." Stevens took a drink. "One girl turned herself in. Calls herself Moonshadow. Came in with a hotshot lawyer a few weeks ago, copped a plea to some old pot charge, did some time and was released this morning. We got a tail on her."

"Where she at?" asked Ra.

"Can't tell you that," said Stevens. That felt good. Keep somethin' from this snitch. Probably should tell him but he don't need to know. He handed Ra the envelope with the cash. "Here's a few thou. Don't go far. We might need you to pick up the trail of that Porgy guy."

"You think he's the one?" asked Ra.

"Somebody does." Stevens didn't know the details of the investigation since it wasn't his baby, but his sixth sense told him that Ra was as likely to be the killer as this other motherfucker. Ra finished his drink and left. Stevens had a couple more. The jukebox continued to play the Temptations.

Fats was in Hawaii living on the beach. No charges had been brought against him or any of the folks at the ranch, but he had to wonder how long that would be the case. Roger was on his way to West Virginia. He had some people there that could hide him out until the shit blew over. The horses would be taken care of. He wondered if torching the place was the right thing to do, but it made sense at the time. They owned the

property so it wasn't like they were fucking with anyone else's cash. Still, it might have attracted unnecessary attention. He had a camp on the beach. The cops
stayed away as long as nobody did anything stupid like
assault or rape. He had to laugh. Eating all the fruit
that grew around them had forced him to lose ten
pounds. Could he still be called Fats?

The Day After Election Day 1980

Iranians were still holding US spies in Tehran. Ronald Reagan the scourge of Berkeley was the new leader. He and Maggie Thatcher wanted to rule the world. The Sex Pistols gone. God bless the fuckin' queen. Peter and moonshadow were on the Greyhound to Oregon. She had been out of prison for a few weeks. The cops ended up keeping her until late September. Said they lost her papers. Peter pulled off a couple deals, finished up the job he had helping a friend hang drywall, and the two of them packed their backpacks, said goodbyes and bought their bus tickets. They hoped they had been careful enough to give the cops the slip. It was obvious moonshadow was being watched. Cars outside the motel. Undercover following her on foot when she went to get coffee. They hadn't even been to Berkeley, but that didn't seem to matter. The SFPD and whoever was helping them were making her and Peter nervous enough.

The bus drove through the night. moonshadow

and Peter were still in love. She rested her head in his
lap. Every once in a while, Peter bent over to kiss her
deeply.

Late May 2007

Santa Rita County Detention. Peter waited for Porgy to come through the gate. The buildings were all new. Solar panels on the roof even. Thirty years ago Peter spent a week in the previous version of these quarters. Drug charges had been dropped and he was let out. Naturally, the place still sucked.

Porgy walked through the gate that opened into the visiting room. Hands cuffed. Legs shackled. He was led to the cubicle where Peter sat. The guard uncuffed his hands. Once sitting, Porgy nodded at Peter. Peter picked up the telephone device. Porgy picked up his.

"Hey."

Peter replied. "Hey. Bummer to see you here."

"Yeah. You look old, man," Porgy cracked.

Peter looked at Porgy. His head was shaved, but he had very few wrinkles. He was a few years older than Peter.

"You lookin' pretty good," said Peter.

"What's it like out there?" asked Porgy. "You know

I been in Mexico for the past several years."

"Uglier than it did when we was hangin' out."

Porgy looked around. He noticed the guards were down at the end of the room shooting the shit with some pretty looking woman from outside.

"I can't believe I'm relivin' this shit," he said. "Where that sumbitch Ra at? That motherfucker got away with somethin'. Murder or whatever, but somethin'."

"Don't know but I aim to find out." Peter looked at Porgy. "You still smoke?"

"No. You can bring me some books though." Porgy shuffled his arms around. He looked over at the guard and leaned into the phone. "What are they sayin'? Can I get out of this?"

Peter answered. "The whole fuckin' reason they got you was because of that story on *America's Most Wanted*. The lawyer doesn't think you did it, especially after I told her the story about Ra and all. She says we'll need lots of proof though because the law wants to put someone away for killing Rosie. In today's paranoid scene you never know what's gonna' happen."

"Let's assume Ra did it. What if he's dead? How do we prove anything?"

"He probably is. That sonofabitch," said Peter.

Porgy clasped his hands and sighed. "What did you think about her anyhow? Rosie, I mean."

Peter thought for a minute or two. "I been thinking about that a lot lately. To put it simply, I have mixed feelings. She was a decent person. But the fact she was a narc still makes me wonder how much of that was an act and how much was really her." He looked at his watch. Five more minutes before the guard cut the visit short. "I'd like to think she was someone who might have come around if she hadn't been killed. My buddy Roger always thought so."

Silence. Porgy thought about his situation. He wasn't pissed off, just frustrated.

"Shit," nodded Porgy. "Whatever happened to Roger?"

"He moved to Nepal. Last I heard he was working construction helping to build hotels for the ecotourists and mountain climbers."

"Sounds like a nice job.. Did you follow that shit about those Maoists over there?" asked Porgy.

"A little," answered Peter. "I never knew exactly what to think of them."

"Me neither. Some of the Mexicans I hung out with in Oaxaca talked about using their process as a model for Mexico. I wasn't convinced it would work anywhere but Nepal."

The buzzer sounded. Time to go. Peter nodded to Porgy. "Later, bro."

June 2007

Peter was online at the library. He'd spent many an hour at the building on University Avenue in Berkeley. He clicked on the website that kept a tally of the Iraq war dead. Four more US soldiers yesterday and god knows how many Iraqis. The fuckin' surge again. He clicked on the *New York Times* site. Immigration raids in the Midwest and south.

There sure was a lot of time and space between his Berkeley days and now.

Peter and moonshadow headed up to to Oregon not long after she did those three weeks. The state's lush green vegetation and the country living did them both good. She even got pregnant but miscarried. That sent her into a tailspin. Too fuckin' bad. After that she seemed to have stopped smiling. Next thing Peter knew she was asking him to drive her to the airport in Portland so she could go back east where her family was. They made some of the best and saddest love Peter had ever partaken in the day before. It was like she wanted to give him everything she had left before she went back to her previous identity. Like she was leaving the person of moonshadow for good. Her belly was still a little round from the pregnancy. He just lay there for hours until she started kissing him again.

The work situation had been bad when they got to Eugene and it just got worse while they lived there. One restaurant job would end and no more would take its place. moonshadow hung out in the house all day beading and smoking weed while Peter took a little bit of work here and a little there. Never enough to do more than sustain the two of them. She told him she felt like she was making him into someone that he wasn't. He said he didn't mind but he knew that he was tired way too much and given to getting pissed at little shit after a week of backbreaking work and hardly any pay. It was hard to let her go and he thought of that drive to the airport often. He still got a postcard from her every once in a while. New York City was the postmark but never a return address. He moved up to the Olympic Peninsula a month or two after she left.

Peter left the library. He was back in People's Park again. Maybe he would run into somebody from the old days. He wanted to find Cat. She might know what the hell happened to Ra. She never trusted him. Her cards might give a clue. She was the only person he could think of that was probably still close to the streets. He still had no clue as to where she might be.

Everyone else had either gone to prison or settled down once they started having kids. His cell phone rang. It was Mariah.

"Hey." he answered.

"Peter..." she sounded a little excited. "Can I meet you for dinner? I got something on Porgy's case."

"Sure. How about Larry Blake's around 6:00? I'm up here already."

"See you in a couple hours, then." Peter closed his cell. He sat on a bench in the park. The bench was at the end that he had helped tear the asphalt from back in 1979. The parties at night during that occupation started off so great. Good food, beer and drugs. People donating trees and tools. Lots of folks bringing eats and energy. The community was truly coming together. After a month the scene slowly disintegrated into a stronghold of the STP family. Their true origins were the stuff of street people legend. Some said the group began when a batch of the hallucinogen STP hit Hippie Hill in San Francisco's Golden Gate Park in 1968 and precipitated a three day freakout and orgy amongst the folk living under the various trees there. Others insisted that the family began in New Mexico at some commune in the desert. Still others claimed Morningstar Farm in the woods north of San Francisco as the Eden for this collection of hustlers, alcoholics, bikers without bikes, and assorted others of mainstream society's outcasts. Although the actual birthplace of the family was in dispute, the role STP played in its creation was never debated. They were mostly good guys but a little too hardened for whatever reasons. Lots of them were Vietnam vets and were still pissed. Some of them were criminals. Some were just drug-addled losers.

The park looked pretty good. Lots of flowers and vegetables. A couple bathrooms and even a swingset. These would last until the next time the university told the cops to destroy them. Then the cops would come swaggering in behind some mercenary's heavy equipment and chase everyone out of the lot so the machines could destroy it again. Fuckin' games about property rights. Peter sipped from a tall boy of beer he kept hidden under his vest.

Around dusk he left the park and headed north on Telegraph to Larry Blake's. He was surprised to see Mariah already there when he walked in. She was sitting with an older professor-looking guy at the bar. Peter walked over and sat on a stool to Mariah's left.

"Hey Peter." Mariah smiled and gave a small wave.

"Hi, Mariah." Peter asked the bartender for a pint of Anchor Steam.

"This is Jim." The two men shook hands. "He was one of my law professors up the street." She nodded toward the UC campus. "Criminal law. He's working on some of the Green Scare cases right now. Providing case law and helping out with other defense issues." The Green Scare involved a series of conspiracy and arson cases brought against a bunch of folks, mostly kids, who were accused of burning down animal research labs. The cases seemed flimsy to Peter but this was the era of the fuckin' Patriot Act, so the state would probably win. The three drank a couple more beers and Jim left, saying something about a wife and kids. Peter and Mariah moved from the bar and found a table tucked in a corner.

Mariah leaned in to Peter. She smiled and pinched his thigh. Peter looked up. She pushed his hair out of his face and kissed him. The kiss lasted several seconds. She handed him a menu.

"What's the big news on Porgy's case?" asked Peter, curiously hopeful about Mariah's friendliness.

"There's a fellow who called me up after you left the other day..," she began. "He was Ra's contact with that time's version of the California Bureau of Investigation. I asked around to verify his credentials. He was definitely the contact. I guess he's dying from cancer and wants to make things right. He told me straight out that he believes Ra was the murderer. He found verification through some contacts he still has that I was handling Porgy's defense. However, he says he doesn't have the proof. At least not yet."

Peter nodded. He had always thought this was the case, but didn't see how it mattered now. "So, how does that help?"

"Well, he's retired now. He wants to come in and talk with me. I set up an appointment for next Monday. I was hoping you could be there."

Peter hesitated. He didn't know how much he wanted to meet some old cop. "If you think it will help."

"I do. If he doesn't want to talk with you there, you can leave and listen to the tape afterwards," Mariah suggested. The waiter came over and they ordered. A couple sandwiches, salads and more drinks.

"I wonder how much help he can provide," said Peter.

"It can't hurt to talk to him." She smiled. After they ate, they went back to Mariah's for the night.

Peter woke up the next morning next to Mariah. She smiled and climbed on top of him.

The following Monday Peter sat in the front room of Mariah's office. The retired cop, who was named Dick Stevens, was in her office with her. He was a black guy. A big guy who looked pretty sick from cancer. They had been talking for over an hour. Peter hoped he had some information. He decided to leave and go for a walk by Lake Merritt. When he came back the cop was gone. Mariah gave him a hug and invited him into the office.

"I recorded the interview," she told Peter. "Tell me what you think." She put the mini-cassette into the small recorder and pushed play.

"My name is Richard Stevens..." the tape began. He continued his introduction, including his agency, the

informants he managed, and the sections he worked in. Finally he began to talk about Porgy's case.

"The informant we all called Ra used to meet me in different bars in Oakland and San Francisco. His given name was Ronnie Freedman. He was originally from Laurel, Mississippi and moved to Los Angeles in 1959 when he was around nine or ten years old with his mother. His father was killed by white men in Mississippi for reasons never explained. Probably some racial element given the time and place. The meetings I am referring to here occurred in the spring of 1980. I met this Ra at least three times during the period I was working with him on the Porgy Johnson case. The first time we met after the murder of McNamara, he was the one who suggested that Johnson was the killer. After claiming that he had been in LA helping his sick mother immediately after the supposed time of McNamara's murder, Ra told the story that he had definitely taken McNamara to the residence in Marin County and dropped her off to make the undercover buy of the LSD. He continued, stating that he then left. According to the informant Ra, the NPLF group had decided that Ra would drop McNamara off and Porgy Johnson would pick her up. This story sounded plausible and I reported it to my superiors, who were also working with the FBI because of McNamara's status as a Federal plant. The next time I met Freedman in the same bar, we discussed the murder of McNamara some more. He had nothing new to add, except that he had heard that Porgy Johnson had headed to the Midwest. In the interim, the Berkeley police had interrogated a woman known on the street as moonshadow. This woman was a member of the NPLF, although according to her statements she

disagreed with their arson. This was the BPD's second interro-gation of this woman. She was already doing a month on a possession charge. When she was asked about the drug deal McNamara was involved in, she stated that Porgy was not in-volved in transporting McNamara at all that night. In fact, she said that Porgy didn't like to drive motor vehicles at all. He preferred bikes. She didn't even know if he knew how to oper-ate a motor vehicle. Although the Berkeley PD had this infor-mation, they didn't share it with my agency until after the aforementioned meeting with the informant Ra.

After my first meeting with Ra after McNamara's murder, the FBI issued an APB for Porgy Johnson. However, he slipped through our fingers, as you well know. I can only wonder at the network involved that got him out of the country. I met with the informant Ra one more time before I was moved to another as-signment. It was in the same bar. I had two thousand dollars to give him from the CBI. We talked a good while about the NPLF---the CHP had arrested two members of the group a week earlier. It was of a couple of females living at a lesbian farm in Humboldt. The arrests were made possible because some pot farmer with a little too much testosterone got threatened by all the dykes on the access road the shared. He made a deal with the CHP to keep his pot if he turned the NPLFers in.

The informant Ra identified the women as members who had participated in the firebombings of the BPD cars. The two ended up copping pleas and did a couple months each. Ra never had to appear in court and blow his cover. Too bad if you ask me. Anyhow, I confronted him with the info I had about Porgy not being the driver that night in Marin. This line was purely my own. The higher-ups were not even considering Ra as a suspect. I never liked the SOB and he just seemed to be the type that would do something like that. I know that is useless in court, but it was in my gut, you know. The guy was a total sleaze. Sell out his fucking mother if he could make some money or dope. He liked the white girls, too. I pushed him on it. Asked him--didn't Rosie want to fuck you, Ra? I had heard that part of this moonshadow's statement included her telling the BPD that Ra had tried to rape her a couple times and that was part of the reason she said she wanted out of the NPLF. But, she said, you can't just leave those kinds of groups. Too much paranoia if you leave at the wrong time. People think you're a cop.

Anyhow, The informer Ra looked at me when I asked if McNamara wouldn't fuck him and did that piss him off? I know you killed her, I said. Look, he said, I may like white girls, but I know you like hookers. I also know that you been taking a cut of the 14th Avenue trade for years. If you try and pin any fuckin' thing on me I'll go to your fuckin' superiors and bust you so bad. I got proof that you don't even know about. I ain't talkin' about hookers telling me that you fucked them or pimps telling me that you kicked the shit out of them for your cut. I'm talkin' about some video I seen of you fuckin' up this one pimp off of Foothill that ended up dying and being left in the street by persons unknown.

Well, when he told me that I knew he had me. When I worked the white slavery beat for the CBI, I got corrupted. I also killed a couple pimps who treated the girls real bad. It was completely extralegal and I would surely do time if I was ever found out. Plus it would ruin my career, my retirement and my marriage. I never mentioned my suspicions about Ra again until now. My wife is dead, I'm old and sick and I got to do what I can. Unfortunately, I don't have any proof. We didn't have DNA testing then. Besides, the evidence for that case went missing. I remember cashing in a favor with the girl in the evidence room. It must have been 1990 or so--several years after most of us figured Johnson was the culprit and that he had fled. I was thinking about the case and decided to pull the stored evidence. It wasn't there. Nothing at all. Zero.

Mariah turned off the recorder. Peter sat still. The mention of moonshadow had brought up some feelings he couldn't describe. He still loved that girl somewhere in his heart. He also loved the times her love represented to him. A certain innocence and hope. Nothing like today when the only hope being talked about was that which one could buy. Or vote for. Which was no hope at all. Mariah took the tape out of the recorder. She put it in her pocket. Her plan was to make a couple copies and place them somewhere safe. The she would see what she had and whether or not it was usable.

Peter stood up. He wanted to go back to his apartment.

"I guess I'll go back to my place."

Mariah looked up from her desk. "You want a ride?"

"Sure, if you're going that way." Peter was surprised at how much moonshadow's memory was affecting him. Mariah and Peter left her office. She grabbed his hand as they left the building and headed to her car.

They drove up Martin Luther King Way. Peter was quiet. Mariah had slipped a Norah Jones CD into the player. The song was Hank Williams' "Cold Cold Heart."

"You obviously don't have one of those," she said to Peter. He looked up. "That moonshadow was an old lover?"

"Yeah. Innocence lost and regained. Those were different times," he said to himself as much as to Mariah. They pulled into the underground garage at the apartment building where Peter was living.

"Can I come in?" asked Mariah. "I've never been."

"Sure, It's kind of empty." They headed upstairs. His apartment was the second door. Peter unlocked the door. Mariah walked in and sat on the couch. Peter went to the fridge and grabbed a couple beers. "You want one?"

Mariah took the beer Peter offered. He sat next to her and she laid her head on his lap.

"So what does this mean? asked Peter. "Can it help Porgy?"

"Depends if we can find any corroboration," replied Mariah. "Even then it could be our witnesses' word against the prosecutor's evidence and the jury's prejudice."

Peter thought about moonshadow. Would she be willing to dredge up this part of her past?

"Your old girlfriend..," Mariah looked at Peter. "Do you keep in touch?"

"I get a postcard every once in a while. No return address on it but always a Manhattan postmark."

"We could try to hunt her down. When was the last time you got one of those cards?"

Peter thought. "2001. Before 9-11."

"See what you can do. What was her name?"

"I knew her as moonshadow. Hippie name she had out here. I think her given name was Linden Epstein. Common Jewish surname. Maybe it was Goldstein."

"Like I said. We can try."

"How much time we got?"

"The DA wants to set a trial date for late July."

It was June 20th.

July 7th. The Fourth of July had been a typical Bay Area celebration. Beer, weed, a chicken and tofu barbecue at a house owned by a Bonita and Arlo--a couple of Peter's oldest friends in the Oakland Hills. A brother brought some barbecue and vodka. Screwdrivers for those who wanted to forget how little freedom there really was anymore. Mariah showed up with a couple other lawyers. One was getting ready to retire and become a painter. The other was working on the San Francisco 8 case. Mostly he was doing research and tracking down witnesses. Not an easy job he said. Most of the folks who were in the armed struggle back in the 1960s and '70s were now either too successful to get involved in a better-off-forgotten part of their past, too drugged out, or in prison and not willing to incriminate themselves in anything that might keep them there past their current sentence. The prosecutors were being real hard asses and were not interested in giving any defense witnesses any kind of immunity. They were intent on railroading the Eight, fuck the Bill of Rights. The more Peter listened the more disillusioned he got about Porgy's chances. He began to hit the screwdrivers harder. A guy who lived next door tossed a couple hits of acid into the screwdriver pitcher. After that, only Peter and the acid provider continued to drink the orange juice and vodka concoction. It had been ten years since Peter's last trip. Too many other things to do and not enough reason to put his mind in that place, even though it was a place he had enjoyed all too frequently a few decades earlier. The jingle jangle as the acid came on was as familiar as the taste of toothpaste in the morning. The brain was a curious thing as it found the grooves worn into Peter's brain so many years ago. As the sun went down over the bay the sound of the goats kept up the road by the city of Oakland to maintain the very flammable grass of the Oakland Hills grew louder. Bleat bleat. The sky began to light up with faraway fireworks and a purple glow. The Coltrane on the stereo melded into the conversation around him. Bonita came outside with a pitcher of sangria. Conversation drifted back to the past when Bonita and Arlo first came to California. Arlo was working construction in

Huntington Beach. Bonita was visiting Peter and Lucy in the northern half of the state. They drove down for a rock festival. After an extended bout of intoxication, Arlo and Bonita disappeared. They came out of a tent the next day. Arlo quit his job, packed up his meager belongings and went back east. Lucy left Peter six months later. By then Bonita was a few months pregnant. After a few years on the east coast, Arlo and Bonita moved to the Bay Area. Arlo was a skilled carpenter by then and opened his own business. Now he had a few select clients that paid lots of money for his unique style of craftsmanship. Peter had been out of touch with the two until the internet came along.

He and Mariah crashed in the extra bedroom at the house. Mariah hadn't eaten acid. They spent most of the night making love. In between, Mariah asked questions. Had Peter ever been married? Did he have kids? Peter answered no to the first and yes to the second.

"Where is he or she?" asked Mariah as she ran her forefinger across his lips. Peter didn't know. It had been a few months since he had heard. "I think she's in Vermont," he said. "Her name is Leda. She was living with a guy near Killington. She works on the ski patrol. Sometimes she's in New England and sometimes she's out west."

"How old is she?"

"Twenty-five." Peter could feel the acid effects leaving his body. He felt fairly relaxed overall. "Her mom and I stayed together for six years after she was born."

He sat up on the futon they were on.

Mariah climbed up on Peter. "What happened?"

"Nothing. We just got tired of each other that way. We raised Leda together but had our own lives." They began to kiss again.

Peter vaguely recalled that moonshadow had told him once about a coop apartment her parents owned on the west side of Manhattan. Somewhere around Ninth Avenue and 25th Street. He was going through the Manhattan phone book and calling every Epstein and Goldstein with an address near there. No luck yet. They had talked about moving there after she got pregnant. Then the miscarriage. She was inconsolable after that. The person that was moonshadow retreated back into the shell she had spawned herself from. Although he had had a couple interesting conversations nothing in the way of a lead had come up.

Three hours later and still calling.

Mariah set her laptop on the table. She reached into her bag and retrieved a CD-R. After turning on the laptop, she put the CD-R in the laptop and waited while the file appeared on a screen. A couple more clicks and an image appeared onscreen. Notes taken on official stationery. California Bureau of Investigation printed across the top. Peter scanned the material. Informant Ronnie Freedman ....

"What this says," began Mariah. "Is that this guy you all called Ra was a longtime informant for the

CBI, FBI and DEA. He was involved not only in drug cases, but also in infiltrating various political groups and gangs. The Panthers, the Crips, and deals with Nicaraguans that were connected to the contras of Nicaragua. No wonder he never got prison for his transgressions. He knew too much."

Peter was clicking through the document. Each time he hit the forward arrow at the top of the reader he saw something else that might one time have surprised him. Some time before COINTELPRO and the Patriot Act. Some time before Porgy got set up. Some time before he found out that the leader of the anti-war group he had been involved with in Vermont was working for the state police. Some time before nothing the government did surprised him. Neither did the lack of genuine reaction from the populace.

...Informant Freedman was reassigned to San Francisco Area. After being arrested by Orange County sheriffs in a domestic abuse case. Search of the victim's premises (Name deleted), one-half ounce of cocaine was found. Freedman arrested. CHP took over case. Case dropped. There were a few such instances in the file Peter read.

Porgy's Fourth of July had nothing to do with independence. He sat in Santa Rita listening to the young wannabes talk their shit. Bitch this and bitch that. They talked like gangsters but had no gangs. It was Porgy's opinion that they were more ignorant then he and his bros had ever been. As for politics--they

didn't exist for these guys. Even most of the young-
sters that knew about the Panthers thought they were
some kind of gang. Of course, thought Porgy, Huey
hadn't helped that perception much. Then again, neither did the schools or even the old brothers and sisters who never talked about that shit any more. He
recalled something he had learned by Frederick Doug-
lass while teaching at the Panther school. What to the
slave is the Fourth of July...? As evening fell, the
sounds of fireworks filtered through the quiet din of
the prison. Porgy remembered those first days of
freedom after Peter and the rest got him out of the
country. Down in Oaxaca with some German folks.
Laying low. Plenty of time for reflection. Plenty of
time to become his new identity.

One of those German women fell in love with him.
And he with her. Two kids later. Both of them living
illegally in Mexico. It was the kids that changed him
the most. He did most of the parenting while their
mom worked at the cafe. They were grown now. One
had made her way into the United States and obtained
a green card. He hadn't heard from her in several
months. He hoped he could see her but didn't want
her to be deported because she was his kid. So he
waited for a response from his ex regarding their
daughter's whereabouts. He hadn't meant to lose track
of the kids but he had been rootless since he left the
ranch in Oaxaca a year and a half ago. If he hadn't
coincidentally been at his ex's right after his mother

died he would never have known. Of course, he wouldn't be in prison waiting trial either.

Porgy thought again about his current neighbors. Many of them were barely twenty-five years old but had spent half their lives incarcerated. He was quite lucky in comparison. This was the longest stint he had ever done. If he added up all the rest of the time including the time in the stockade it probably came to three years at the most. That was peanuts compared to many black men.

Dreams of his own death had haunted Porgy's sleep since he was sent to Santa Rita. Occasionally brutal but more often his expiration came quietly in those dreams with Porgy waking just before the end. In all his time on the run he had never dreamed of his own death.

Peter was back at the apartment. He was reading a newsletter from the SF 8 Defense Committee. Had there been any point to all those politics back then? Peter couldn't help but wonder. Porgy in prison over something he didn't do. And he was just one of dozens. Every couple months Peter received an email from a group called the Jericho Movement that detailed the fate of the men and women they called prisoners of war. Essentially, these were men and women who had been involved in the liberation and revolutionary movements of the 1960s and 1970s and were doing time. Some had actually committed crimes and some were victims of the police state. No matter what, it often seemed like the fascists had won.

The trial was in ten days. They still had very little in Porgy's defense. moonshadow seemed to have dropped from the earth. He had no luck in finding her. Now he wished he had met her parents. But that wasn't how it worked then. Hell, he still wasn't even sure of her given name. Mariah was considering trying to convince Porgy to cop a plea. Peter doubted that he would.

A Week Before Trial, Late July 2007

Unable to do much about his present, Porgy mostly thought about his past. He didn't dare hope about his future, if any. He still had only two regrets concerning his past. That he had killed people in Southeast Asia and that he had come back to the States in 2007. His timing could not have been worse.

Mariah waited in the prison's visitors room. Porgy was led out by a guard. He sat down. The expression on her face was not a good one. He didn't know what that meant. The last time they talked she was hyped up because of some old cop's testimony about Ra. While it proved what Porgy always figured--that Ra was an informer--it didn't prove Porgy's innocence. And no one knew where Ra was.

"Hi Porgy." Mariah smiled.

"Hey."

"No good news, but we have to talk about some things." Mariah wasn't sure how to breach the subject of a plea bargain. Porgy could sense what was coming.

He looked at her.

"I ain't coppin'," he told her. "I didn't do the crime."

"I hate to be saying this," she began. "But look at what you're facing and at least think about it."

Porgy looked away. He could not remember ever feeling so powerless. Not even when he was hiding out at the marina. He looked at his lawyer. "Go ahead."

"Okay." Mariah took out her notes. "We have the retired cop's testimony. If he is well enough to appear in court he will. Otherwise all we have is his taped deposition. We don't have anyone to verify his testimony or match what it says. Peter has been unable to find his old girlfriend. We believe Ra is dead, but the DA will not release that information and all of our attempts to uncover it have been met with flat out statements that those files are no longer around. The current climate in the courts are not hospitable to political radicals of any kind. If you plead to manslaughter, I can probably get you a maximum sentence of fifteen."

"I can't do it," insisted Porgy. "I didn't do the fuckin' crime." It wasn't fear of prison but the anger at doing time that prevented him from considering any type of deal.

Mariah looked away. She believed him and felt like a criminal asking him to even consider such a route. She pulled another file of papers from her bag.

An alarm sounded. Immediately, the guards announced visiting was over and began to lead the prisoners back to their cells. Armed men in uniforms approached the visitors with their hands on their night-sticks. Mariah flashed Porgy a peace sign. "Let me know." The guards began rushing the visitors out of the building as quickly as they could. Lockdown. Sheriff's deputies in SWAT gear were gathering in the parking lot. Guns in the hands of all the guards. Shotguns and semiautomatics. Making mental notes to herself regarding the guns and flurry of movement, Mariah got in her car and drove a short distance off. She called Peter on her cell.

Peter answered. He was at home watching the A's play Minnesota. Mariah had lent him a TV.

"Peter!" Mariah sounded a bit apprehensive. "Turn on the radio or TV or something."

"I have the ball game on." He told her. "Why? What's up?"

"The prison just went into a lockdown. I was visiting Porgy. I need to find out what's going on."

Peter began surfing through the channels. Nothing. He turned on the radio and began scanning the dial. Nothing there either. "Where are you?" He hoped she wasn't in the prison.

"I'm about a mile from the prison. They made all of us leave. I drove a short ways and pulled off the road," she explained. "There were at least a hundred Alameda deputies and others in the parking lot when I was thrown out. All in full SWAT gear. Guns everywhere."

"What about Porgy?" Peter hoped the cops didn't know what Porgy was in for although he figured they probably did.

"He was taken away. He didn't act like he knew what was going on."

Peter wondered. A news flash began to run across the bottom of the screen. "Wait, Mariah. Here's something. Let me read it. Alameda County corrections officials tell Channel Four News that unrest has broken out at Santa Rita Correctional Facility near Pleasanton. Police and corrections guards are attempting to pacify the situation right now. More news at 11."

"I'm going to stay here until I hear something more. I'll keep in touch." She hung up.

Inside the prison, two blocks were unguarded. A group of prisoners held several guards hostage. The group of prisoners that included Porgy had been removed from the visitors room and were being held in a corridor that was double-locked on both ends. They were shackled and handcuffed. There was a chain link fence above them. In essence, they were in a cage. The SWAT team was awaiting orders to enter the prison while guards inside secured the remaining blocks. An hour passed. The sound of the riot came and went. Porgy could see the visitors room filling up with cops in armor, tear gas masks, assault rifles and grenade launchers. A couple of the men in the corridor were getting claustrophobic and pulling on the chains that shackled all of the men together. One of the cops from outside stood at the end of the corridor with his shotgun trained on the men in the corridor. Another stood behind him with a tear gas gun. The door was open and all that separated the guards from the prisoners were two gates made from chain link fence that stretched from the floor to the ceiling.

Mariah was still in her car. The lights were off. Her line to Peter was open. He relayed what he could glean from the news reports. Details were sketchy. More police agencies rolling in. Two blocks erupted into violence. Might have been caused by gang rivalries. Mariah watched a steady stream of police and news vehicles head towards the prison. She hoped she was hidden well enough so no one would tell her to leave.

Forty minutes passed. A large amount of tear gas was floating in the yard and the two unsecured blocks. Porgy could hear shouts and the sound of beatings from where he was shackled. He wondered once again why he didn't stay in Mexico. Suddenly, the men in the corridor heard several loud and very rapid pops. The prisoner shackled to Porgy on his right said quietly, "Assault weapons." A guard in the visitors room fired a tear gas canister into the corridor. The men began choking. Another canister landed in the corridor. Porgy fell, gasping for air. He felt a tightness in his chest and collapsed on the floor. The other men collapsed soon afterwards.

Mariah was on the phone. "There must be at least three or four hundred cops in there by now. Plus the guards. It certainly doesn't look good." She watched more law enforcement vehicles drive toward the prison. Emergency vehicles too.

"The news seems to have stopped," reported Peter. "The television's gone back to its regular shows and even KPFA doesn't have any info. I'll keep you posted."

"Thanks."

"Hey," Peter was thinking out loud. "Don't you think you might be better off coming back here?"

"No. I want to be the first one in once they end this thing." She took a deep breath. "I don't feel good about what's going down in there."

"Prison is never good," agreed Peter.

"I'll keep in touch." Mariah closed her cell phone. She decided to try and sleep for a few minutes. It was around one in the morning. She put her seat back and dozed off. The sound of her ring tone woke her. It was 3 AM.

"Hey." It was Peter.

"Any news?" asked Mariah.

"No." Peter sounded relieved. "Just checkin' in. I fell asleep."

"Me too." Mariah put her seat back in an upright position. "I think I'll wait until it starts to get light and go back up to the prison. Maybe they'll let me in."

"Turn on your radio." The two of them listened to KPFA from their respective posts. No real news. She turned hers to an all-news station. After a few minutes of commercials, she heard what she wanted. According to officials, the situation was under control. All of the prisoners were back in their cells and the prison was secure.

"I wonder how many are dead," said Peter.

"I'm going up there now." Mariah hung up the phone and started her car. The sky was turning blue. She pulled on to the access road heading to the prison. She ran into a police roadblock set up about a quarter mile from the main gate.

"Hello ma'am." an Alameda County Sheriff holding a shotgun leaned in her window. "No one is permitted to go any further. However, I need to see your identification?"

Mariah had her license at the ready. She handed it to the cop. He took the license to his car and called it in to dispatch. Mariah waited. The deputy came back and handed her license back to her.

"I'm an attorney," she began. "One of my clients is inside."

"You'll have to wait like everyone else." The deputy pointed to a field off the road where five or six other cars and some news trucks were parked.

"How long?" asked Mariah.

"I don't know, ma'am." Mariah parked her car near the others and got out. She headed towards the KOMO-TV news truck. Perhaps her friend Jasmin was working this story. The rear door to the truck opened as Mariah got near. A Latino woman with a camera stepped down and waved.

"Hey Mariah." It was Jasmin. "What are you doing here?"

Mariah looked around to make sure no police could hear her. "I was in the prison when this started," she told Jasmin. "One of my clients was hustled off from the visitors room and they rushed us out the door. I want to know what happened to him."

Jasmin nodded. "We haven't heard a thing since about 1:30," she told Mariah. "That's when the scanner went dead. Right after a bunch of commands to go in and take the remaining cell blocks. I have a feeling it isn't pretty inside."

Mariah didn't say anything. It didn't sound good. "So you don't have any word on when they'll re-open?"

"All we know is that the officials are saying the situation is resolved. I'm guessing they'll have a news conference around 7 or 8 this morning." Jasmin reached into the truck for a sweater and put it on. "You all right?"

"Yeah, I could use some coffee, though," answered Mariah.

"We got some coming." Jasmin looked around. "You want to sit in the truck? It's just me and my sound guy, Nguyen."

"Yeah, thanks." The two women climbed into the truck and pulled the door closed. Mariah sat on a cushion and leaned back, hoping to grab another few minutes of sleep.

"Tell me a little about your client. Off the record."

7:30 AM. Word was that prison officials and the

Sheriff's department would be talking to the press in half an hour. Mariah was still in the truck with Jasmin. The coffee had come along with some donuts. She felt awake. The news truck was getting crowded as the equipment was taken out and set up. Mariah went back to her car and climbed inside. She turned on the radio and called Peter.

"Hey," Peter answered immediately. "What's going on?"

"There's going to be a news conference in a few minutes."

"How you doing?" asked Peter. "Did you get any sleep?"

"Yeah." Mariah smiled to herself. It was nice that this man cared. "I'm feeling okay. If you can, tape the news conference. I'll be at your place soon."

"Talk to you soon then." Peter hung up.

The cameras and microphones were ready. A black car with Department of Corrections markings on it had just pulled into the field where the other vehicles were parked. The sun was warming up the air. Two men got out of the black car and talked to one of the deputies. The deputy led one of the men to the microphones. Mariah made her way to the front of the small crowd of reporters. Some had microphones, some pencil and papers and some had Blackberries or iPhones.

"First," the speaker began. "Let me reassure the citizens of Alameda County that the situation at the detention facility is under control. The rioting prisoners have been subdued and are back in their cells. Alameda County deputies are supplementing Corrections employees in cleaning up the prison and administering medical care to those who need it. No outside visitors will be allowed into the prison until further notice. In addition, no new prisoners will be admitted at this time. We are currently working with local and state officials to find spaces for those individuals. It is with no small regret that I have to tell you that, as of approximately half an hour ago, there are five fatalities. One was a corrections guard who had worked at this prison for fifteen years. The other four were inmates. We will release the names of these individuals once their next of kin is notified.

It is the duty of the Corrections Department to keep prisoners away from the non-prison population and to keep both populations safe. I believe that the way our officers handled last night's disturbances was a fine example of the department's (and the individuals in the department) dedication to this mission. We are investigating the causes of the disturbances and the authorities handling of it. Once a full report is written, we will share it with the public. Thank you."

The official left the microphones and returned to his car, ignoring all questions. Mariah waited until the official car left, headed over to hers, got in and drove away.

She spent the next two days at Peter's. She called the office occasionally. They ate pizza and takeout.

They drank wine. They followed the news about the prison. Very little information was forthcoming. Just like in Iraq and Afghanistan, the powers that be knew how to control information. The fact that most media members seemed okay with this state of affairs pissed Peter off to no end. By the third day, Mariah was ready to go back to the office.

No sooner had she entered the front doom of her office when the receptionist told her to call Jasmin. Mariah went into her office, closed the door and dialed.

"Jasmin?"

"Hey Mariah." Jasmin sounded like she always did, cool, calm and collected. "I've got some info for you."

Mariah grabbed a pencil and a scrap of paper. "I'm ready."

"The names of the dead." Jasmin waited. "One of them is your client."

"You sure?" asked Mariah. "Porgy Johnson?"

""Yeah." Jasmin heard Mariah gulp for breath. "You all right?"

"Any info on cause of death?"

"No," responded Jasmin. "This list just came through and I happened to be around when it did."

"Thanks." Mariah had a feeling she would get this news herself soon.

"If I get anything more, I'll pass it on," Jasmin told her.

"Great. Later."

Mariah called Peter and told him the news.

The line was quiet.

Peter was at Mariah's place. He could see Lake Merritt down below. It was morning. A week had passed since the news about Porgy. They still didn't know the cause of death. Mariah had a friend in the Sheriff's department looking into it but was told that any info regarding the riot was difficult to find. Something was going on, but nobody who cared knew what. And there weren't too many people that cared. Mariah was in court. Peter debated going for a walk around the lake or staying inside.

It wasn't that he felt he had failed Porgy. Hell, he had done all he could to get him out of the country the first time he was wanted for the murder. He didn't think they were much closer to proving his innocence in 2007 than in 1980. But there was hope. Something that had been in short supply in 1980 where Porgy was concerned. Or maybe that hope was mere illusion. The question was: could he and Mariah somehow clear his name? Or, at the least, find out how he died?

August 2007

Peter was at the Berkeley Flea Market with Mariah. He heard someone say--Is that Peter? He turned toward the voice. A blond woman stood there. It was Rain. Or at least that's what she called herself the last time he had seen her--probably in 1979.

"Hey!" They hugged.

"What the hell?" Peter smiled. "How you been?"

"I'm doing good. What are you doing here?" shouted Rain. "I haven't heard nothing about you in years. You look the same though."

Mariah was bargaining with some rasta guy over some clothing. Peter and Rain caught up. She was driving for AC Transit and sold car parts and tools almost every weekend at the Flea Market.. Rain looked at her cell and said she had to leave. They traded cell numbers.

"Whatever happened to Nathaniel?" asked Peter.

"He got into crack," said Rain. "Ended up doing some time. He's out now. I see him on the bus every once in a while."

"Give him my number."

"I will. See you around." They hugged. Rain walked toward the BART station.

Nathaniel was the quintessential street freak. If the Hog Farm and other communes were communities of freaks who lived in an alternative reality that they helped create, Nathaniel was the loner in the picture. He left Ohio for the Haight-Ashbury when he was fourteen. He arrived just in time for the first of many police crackdowns and hippie riots in 1967. Since riots weren't what he came to California for, he got in a couple licks and headed across the bay to Berkeley and Telegraph Avenue. Life was a bit easier there since it was still relatively undiscovered turf. With his young good looks and a considerable amount of charm his life was pretty much work-free. Doors which were already cracked in the cultural revolution opened wide for Nathaniel. Politics were peripheral in his life except when they affected his ability to operate independently, like the war and police harassment did. People's Park put it all together. When the cops closed the park down his life was threatened and, like so many others, he fought back although he would have preferred to just continue getting high with one or more of his many girlfriends. Self defense was what the battle was about, he had told Peter many years ago as they sat in a friend's van getting high while the kid he was parenting played in the nearby woods of Monte Rio—his temporary refuge from the streets of Berkeley. Streets where he gathered change from passersby as regularly as many of them went to work.

"Who was that?" asked Mariah. She had a bag with the skirt in it. They headed to a booth where a fellow sold Jamaican food.

"One of the first people I met when I got to Berkeley," answered Peter. "She was a runaway fifteen year old then in love with a sixteen year old dyke. Goes by the name of Rain. I honestly thought she'd be dead by now."

"That's kind of cruel!" said Mariah.

"No," answered Peter. He gave the foodseller five bucks and took a plate of food. "The last I heard she was strung out on crack. It hit Telegraph Ave. hard."

"Yeah. Even Marin got nailed by that shit," said Mariah. Peter gave the guy another five and he handed Mariah another plate of food. They headed to a curb to sit and eat.

"Do you like my new skirt?" she asked, holding it up to her body.

"Very much so...," Peter took her plate of food, set it on the curb and pulled her into his lap. They kissed. "When we're done eating let's go to my place."

Mariah smiled.

Monday morning. The weekend had been pleasant. After the flea market they went to Peter's and spent the afternoon naked. That evening they went dancing at a blues club in Oakland. Sunday was spent in San

154

Francisco. Mariah was at her office and Peter was back on Telegraph. He was still hoping to run into Cat or maybe Nathaniel. Who knew? They might have something he could use.

A table was set up at the top of Bancroft. A couple dozen people stood around it arguing and gesturing. Peter walked toward the scene. The banner hanging in front of the table read College Republicans. Peter laughed. Times did change. Even in the late 1970s one never saw Republicans being so brazen in Berkeley. An attractive young woman handed him a leaflet. It advertised a film showing. The film was some kind of rightwing attack film on Islam and the US Left. Republicans were prettier than he remembered thought Peter. He drifted in closer to the arguments. The rightwingers were outnumbered but they were holding their own. Until one of them pushed a young hippie-looking guy in the chest. He fell down and the arguing turned into a fight. Within seconds, the UC cops were there, pushing everyone away from the table except, amazingly, the people who were running it. No arrests were made. The cops stood in front of the table. They looked like they had no intention of leaving. Instead, almost everyone else did.

Peter turned around and headed back down Telegraph. He stopped at Blondie's Pizza for a slice and some juice. While he waited he saw Bonita. He waved. She came over.

"Hey," She hugged him. "What's up?"

"I'm kind of hoping I'll run into Cat or maybe even Nathaniel. I saw Rain the other day."

"Wow." Bonita knew Rain from the long ago days. "I thought she was dead."

"That's what I said to Mariah," said Peter.

"You still hanging out with her?"

"Yeah. She's all right." Peter took his slice from the counter girl. He and Bonita went outside.

"She's quite pretty, too," agreed Bonita. "You all should come over for dinner. I'll talk to Arlo and set a date."

"Cool." Peter finished his slice and threw away the paper.

"Was your friend in that thing out at Santa Rita?" asked Bonita. "It sounded pretty fucked up."

"Yeah," Peter swallowed. "He died."

"I'm so sorry, Peter." Bonita hugged him tightly.

"We're trying to find out what happened," said Peter. "But nobody is saying very much."

"Arlo and I were talking about it," said Bonita. "He was saying that it might have started as some kind of gang thing, but the cops probably used it to get rid of some people they didn't like. Did you see on the news that two of the dead guys were supposedly big time gang leaders that were gonna' testify about police involvement in the crack and heroin trade?"

"Yeah." Peter was quiet. "It makes you wonder why Porgy got it though. He wasn't even in the country until a few months ago."

"Maybe they were just paying him back for what they think he did."

"Yeah," said Peter. "Maybe."

"Or maybe it was an accident," said Bonita. "A real one."

Later That Month

Arlo and Peter were at the A's game. The A's were playing the Blue Jays. A friend of Arlo's had season tickets right behind the A's dugout and was out of town. She had given them to Arlo. The A's weren't looking particularly good, but it was a baseball game in Oakland. Those were always a blast. Peter had spent many an afternoon in the bleachers back in the 1970s when bleacher seats were two dollars and a person could bring in their own beer. Lots of weed was smoked up in those seats back then. Now, baseball was a family affair. At least the stadium still had its paintings of Jerry Garcia and other Bay Area notables over some of the entrances.

The two men were working on some microbrews. The last house Arlo had finished was owned by some kind of magnate who owned an interest in some aspect of the stadium operations and had given Arlo a card that was essentially a ticket for as much free beer and food as he wanted. So they were taking advantage of the offer. The game was beginning. DiNardo was pitching against Halladay. It looked like a certain win for the visitors. However, by the end of the first inning the A's were ahead two to nothing. Arlo took his baseball seriously and rarely talked while the players were on the field. After the first inning, he looked over at Peter.

"Do you remember that girl I met at that rock festival in Pennsylvania? Her name was Marion. About ninety pounds, long black hair and maybe five feet tall."

"Yeah. She came back to our house in Maryland, right?"

"Yeah," said Arlo. "Then her and I drove to Virginia and I got busted for not moving at a green light."

"Yeah," agreed Peter. "What about her?"

"I ran into her out here a couple weeks ago."

"Did she remember you?" Peter asked, wondering if Bonita might get a little jealous.

"Yeah. She's recently divorced. Still pretty. She was with her ex-- this guy named Michael. They were eating dinner at an Italian place on College where I stopped in for takeout. I met him and talked for a while," answered Arlo. "Some silicon valley guy who said he used to live in Berkeley and left in 1980. I asked him where he lived back then and he said on San Pablo. He's supposed to be at the game today. I told him I'd look him up."

"Where are his seats?" asked Peter.

"On the first base side up about thirty rows is what he said. I have his cell number, so I'll just call him.

Might as well get him a beer."

Arlo pushed in the numbers on his cell. He waited. DiNardo got the third out of the inning. "Hey, Michael. Arlo here. What's up?" Peter watched a couple kids in front of him eat their hot dogs. Arlo hung up his phone. He motioned to Peter to follow him. They went to a bar on the right field side of the field. Arlo waved to a big fellow who looked about fifty. Graying hair. Healthy build. Around 200 pounds. Six foot one. Peter felt like he knew the guy. He walked to the bar and Arlo introduced the two of them.

"Michael," he began. "This is my old friend Peter. Peter....Michael."

Michael and Peter shook hands. Michael ordered beers and shots of Makers Mark for the three of them. Peter tossed back his shot. He looked at Michael. The three men traded small talk. Work they were doing. Baseball talk. Kids. Michael ordered three more shots.

When they came, he raised his glass. "To Porgy." Peter looked up. Now he remembered. This was Red Dog from the NPLF. The three men toasted Porgy. "That's where I recognize you from, Red Dog," said Peter.

"Yeah, man" Michael shook Peter's hand again. He smiled. "When Arlo told me a little about you, I knew who you were right off. I was bummed when I heard through the grapevine that Porgy was one of those killed in that fuckin' riot."

"How did you hear?" wondered Peter.

"A black guy I work with whose nephew is in Santa Rita told me that one of the dead was an old dude who was on *America's Most Wanted* for killing some narc back in 1980," answered Michael.

"And?"

"And I put it together that it was Porgy....I saw the *America's Most Wanted* segment he was talking about."

Peter wasn't sure what to say next. Was Michael on the other side--whatever that meant? Or was he still an ally? He figured he would risk asking.

"So what do you think?" he asked.

"I never thought he was the killer," answered Michael. "Even though I gave up that life a long time ago, I still feel he got burned." Michael looked around. He thought to himself that this bar full of wealthy baseball fans and businessmen wasn't the best place to talk about his past revolutionary activities.

"Let's meet over in the bleachers in about twenty minutes. Section 26," suggested Michael. "We can talk some more. "

The three men finished their beers and left.

They met in the bleachers. Michael brought three 24 ounce beers with him. After a couple swallows of beer he began to talk.

"I always wondered what happened to you all," he told Peter. "After the heat died down, I left Oregon and just kind of drifted for about six years. Then my sister died from breast cancer and I went to her funeral. My dad and mom laid a bit of a trip on me, but he used his connections to find out if there were any warrants out on me. There weren't. I went back to school and got into computers. Next thing I know I'm married and living in Cupertino doing software development. Not a bad life, just real different from the one I was living less than ten years before. My wife left four years ago. Our kids are grown. One is married to his boyfriend in San Francisco and the girl is living in Brazil with her boyfriend. Good kids. I wouldn't trade them for anything. Their mom and I get along. She just wanted to be single again"

Peter nodded in recognition. "Sounds like the mother of my kid. I think she's in Germany showing her art."

"So, what are you doing in Oakland, man?" asked Michael.

"I came out here to help Porgy and his lawyer," began Peter. "Then I decided to stay."

"He fell for the lawyer is what happened," laughed Arlo.

Peter laughed. "Yeah. I guess I did. " He tossed back the beer. "But we're also trying to get Porgy's name cleared and find out what happened in that prison that got him killed."

"Good luck on that," responded Michael. "These cops nowadays don't like to admit anything."

"We're finding that out," said Peter, referring to his and Mariah's efforts.

"Look, man," said Michael. "If I can help in anyway that doesn't involve my name getting in the mix, let me know. If the wrong people find out my past I'm a goner."

Peter looked up. His first thought was who cares. Then, he realized that Michael's money could be useful. Plus, he could respect his desire not to bring up what was really ancient history--especially in America-- the land of the thirty minute memory. He told Michael that he would be in touch. They sat back and watched the game. Some reliever named Casilla was pitching for the A's. The score was tied. The Jay's pitcher Halladay was still in.

After the game Michael gave Peter his email and a promise to bring by a couple thousand in cash to help out.

Hunter's Point Weekly

September 9, 2007

Death of A Revolutionary
by Merillee Jackson

The recent prison disturbance at Alameda County's Santa Rita County Jail may have taken the community by surprise, but it did not surprise those closest to the daily goings-on at the facility. Lawyers, corrections officers, relatives of inmates and recently released inmates all agree that the jail was nearing a boiling point this past summer. A combination of cutbacks, staff working too much overtime, a crackdown on petty criminals throughout Alameda County, and a simmering gang war all contributed to the six hour riot.

Although officials are reluctant to release many details of the incidents that occurred that night or in the days preceding it, the public does know this: five men died, forty-one were injured, two cell blocks were destroyed by fire and water, and there was more than $10 million worth of damage to the facility. After the disturbance was quelled, some prisoners were transferred to other jails and prisons in the region, some were given early release, and several dozen are currently living in the prison yard, which has been closed to other prisoners.

What this means is that most inmates at the facility are no longer being let out except for meals. The rest of the day they spend in their cells. Visiting hours have been limited to one weekend a month and worship hours are severely curtailed. According to various guards we interviewed, the place is (according to one anonymous individual) "more tense than before the fuckin' riot."

Correctional officials have released the names of those who died in the riot. A guard named Jerry Hinckle died in the first minutes of the riot. He was apparently killed by unknown prisoners. Two of the inmate dead were well-known gang leaders in the Bay Area named Jesus Aramacio and Bobby Taylor. The two once led rival gangs but in recent years the two gangs have joined forces. Furthermore, *The Weekly* has confirmed what has been rumored for weeks. Both men had agreed with federal officials to testify about police corruption and involvement in the Bay Area drug trade and murder. The other two men were less well-known, at least to today's news readers. One of them called himself Gypsy. He was a white man in his sixties who used to live on the streets of Berkeley and the Haight-Ashbury. A member of the street family known in underground lore as the STP Family, Gypsy spent his last twenty years in prison after being convicted of killing a UC Berkeley student at Barrington Hall--a defunct student co-op that was known by police and Berkeleyites alike as a center for drug dealing, sex orgies and other unconventional (and often illegal) behavior. He was at Santa Rita due to the overpopulation of the state prison system.

The other inmate fatality in the riot was Porgy Johnson. Wanted by federal, state and local law enforcement agencies for more than two decades, Johnson surfaced last spring not long after his case was featured on *America's Most Wanted*. He was awaiting trial on murder charges going back to 1980.

A Radical Past

Porgy Johnston was born in 1950 in San Antonio, Texas. His father was an Air Force NCO. Like most other military families, the Johnsons moved every three or four years. Most of Sergeant Johnson's tours were stateside. He was a plane mechanic and helped keep the Strategic Air Command fighter jets in top condition. In 1962, the family was assigned to Khair Sagalie Air Station near Peshawar, West Pakistan. At the time, Pakistan had two wings. One was between India and Afghanistan and the other was thousands of miles away on India's northeastern flank. The eastern half is now Bangladesh.

The Peshawar air station was a small outpost, known primarily to those who knew it at all as the place where U2 pilot Gary Powers took off from before his ill-fated trip to spy on the Soviets. Perhaps Sergeant Johnson helped maintain the U2s. The family stayed in Peshawar for three years. They were the only African-American family on the base in an Air Force that was primarily white. Porgy used to tell friends of his that *The Weekly* interviewed that his parents used to take him to the Peshawar bazaar at least twice a month. They did this, he said, so that he would know that not everyone in the world was white skinned.

Sergeant Johnston retired from the Air Force in 1969. The family moved to Berkeley, California so that Porgy could attend one of the Bay Area colleges. He was an A student in high school. He didn't go to college after graduating in 1968 because his family didn't know where they would be living after his father's retirement. Instead, Porgy worked at a Sears warehouse in Davis, CA. where his father was stationed.

In 1969, the US Selective Service began using the lottery system. Porgy's number was 17. The draft was finally going to take him. Porgy went in. His father would have disowned him if he hadn't. By March 1970 he was in Vietnam. There was no plane mechanic work for him. He was an infantry man. By May of that year he would find himself in Cambodia, part of the "incursion" ordered by President Nixon. It was a move that unleashed a torrent of rage across the United States. On May 4, 1970 four students were killed by the National Guard during antiwar disturbances there. Ten days later, two more young people were killed in Jackson, Mississippi during similar protests. In between, millions of students walked out of classes, six blacks were killed by law enforcement in Augusta, Georgia and servicemen and women refused to fight or work.

The unrest did not go unnoticed by the young soldier. Several African-American GIs in his unit were regular readers of the Black Panther newspaper. Porgy began to read it himself. By the time he was shipped home in March 1971, he was no longer a good soldier. Indeed, he was no longer a patriotic American. He had joined the Black Panther Party. Within days of his return he spoke at a Panther rally in Berkeley's Provo Park. He called for a revolution and told the crowd he was organizing inside the military. His father died three days after Porgy came back from Vietnam. According to military records, the younger Johnson was sent to Germany in April 1971 after being granted two weeks of bereavement leave. He continued being an active member of the Panthers. According to some former Panther members who lived in Frankfurt am Main, Germany at the time and published the local Panther paper *The Voice of the Lumpen*, Johnson helped organize a speaking tour by Fania Davis, whose sister Angela was on trial for her alleged involvement in an attack on the Marin County Courthouse in 1970. He also played conga in a musical group that played the music of the Last Poets and other revolutionary groups.

After his release from the service, Porgy drifted around Europe. He found his way back to the Bay Area around 1976. The revolutionary fervor was tempered by then, but the street scene on Telegraph Avenue was still going strong. He joined in immediately. Porgy became a well known figure in People's Park, on the Ave, and in various political and countercultural happenings. His mother told *The Weekly* that they read about Porgy in the paper more than they saw him in those days.

In 1978, things took a more serious turn. The SLA and Patti Hearst were a thing of the past. The Weather Underground was a memory to anyone but the most hardened leftist and the Black Panther Party was an occasional electoral phenomenon in Oakland city elections. Porgy ran into a group of young men and women who were still revolutionary. They called themselves the New Peoples Liberation Front (NPLF). Some of the individuals had tenuous ties to the SLA and the others had connections to the Berkeley radical scene. Porgy ran into a member in Peoples Park and soon moved into the house

the group rented on San Pablo Avenue in Berkeley. According to observers of US radicalism
in the 1960s and 1979s, the group was different
from other similar formations primarily because
it did not form until 1977. This was after most
radical organizations were either foundering,
involved in organizing in factories, or, in the
case of the Weather Underground, disintegrat-
ing in a final internal battle.

What Porgy and the other members didn't
know was that the group was infiltrated. Not by
one agency, but by two. There was a man named
Ronnie Freedman (known as Ra) who worked
for the California Bureau of Investigation (CBI)
and the FBI. There was a woman named Rosa
McNamara (Rosie) who also worked for the
CBI, as well as the DEA. Neither undercover
agent knew about the other. The group showed
up at protests against slumlords like the Berkeley Judge who tried to evict the White Panther
Party from their Berkeley housing and issued
statements that were occasionally published in
the final issues of the *Berkeley Barb*. However,
most of their time was spent earning money to
pay their rent and honing the politics of the
group. There was also a fair amount of sexual
experimentation among most of the group's
members.

Murder, Molotovs and Murder

In 1979, the Berkley police killed a popular
street figure named Thomas Africa. The murder

occurred in a climate of increased police harassment of the street people and culture in Berkeley. The campaign was part of an attempt to
rid the city of elements considered repulsive to
the real estate and other industries. There was a
stepped-up police presence on Telegraph Avenue. Concerts in People's Park were broken up
by the police. When the University tried to turn
the parking lot in the west end of the park into
a pay parking lot, the asphalt was torn up and a
three month confrontation between denizens of
the park, their supporters and the police and
university took place. It could be argued that the
protesters won, as the University did not try to
develop the park for more than a dozen years
afterwards.

The NPLF decided they would respond to the
police killing of Africa. On December 19, 1979,
they tossed Molotov cocktails into the parking
lot where Berkeley Police kept their vehicles.
Three vehicles burned. Because of the infiltration
of the group, the police knew who the perpetra-
tors were almost immediately. They decided not
to act, however. It seems that one of the
informants--a woman named Rosie McNamara--
was also involved in trying to take down a LSD
distribution ring operating in Marin County. In
February 1980, the other informant (Ra) (neither
individual was aware of the other's police role)
dropped her off near the house where she was
supposed to buy the LSD. Two weeks later her

corpse was found on the side of I-680 just past San Quentin.

Within weeks, Porgy Johnson was the number one suspect for the crime. His friends at the time insisted that he was not the culprit. Those who hoped to represent him in the trial he will never attend insist the same.

The Facts

After conversations with Johnson's lawyer , a retired undercover agent for the political and gang wing of the State of California's Bureau of Investigation (CBI), and a friend of Johnston's, *The Weekly* summarizes the case below.

June 23. 1979: Thomas Africa killed by Berkeley Police on Telegraph Avenue.

December 19, 1979: NPLF firebombs Berkeley Police cars in response to the murder of Africa.. Three cars destroyed. NPLF claims responsibility in a statement reported by radio station KPFA.

March 1980: Undercover policewoman Rosie McNamara's body found in Marin County. Apparent homicide and sexual assault. Large amounts of barbiturates found in her bloodstream. Police tell public they are searching for two African-American men.

April- June 1980: NPLF members go underground. Porgy Johnson becomes prime suspect in murder of McNamara. His name is put on the FBI's Most Wanted list. He disappears into Mexico. Johnson assumes the identity Esteban

Cruz. The other suspect (Ra) is apparently removed from consideration. According to retired agent Richard Stevens, this individual, referred to as Freedman in defense documents, was known to most of his acquaintances as Ra. He was a long time informant for a number of California police agencies, including the LAPD, CHP, and the Berkeley and Oakland Police departments. Stevens believes to this day that Freedman was the murderer.

February 17, 2007: *America's Most Wanted* features the murder of Rosie McNamara and the disappearance of the "number one suspect in the case, Porgy Johnson" on its show. Johnson is assumed to still be somewhere in Mexico.

March 17, 2007: Johnson attends his mother's funeral in Oakland, California. Police arrest him soon afterwards in traffic stop..

Early April 2007: Attorney Mariah Callahan is assigned to Johnson's case as a public defender. She struggles with the case due to a paucity of information.

Early May, 2007: Peter Somers, a former friend of Johnson's and other NPLF members, receives letter from Callahan asking for assistance. Somers flies to Berkeley to help out.

July 23, 2007: During a visit with Johnson, Callahan and other visitors are hastily removed from the Santa Rita Jail grounds after a disturbance breaks out. The disturbance spreads. The facility is calm by morning. Four inmates die during the disturbance. Johnson is one of them.

The End

Nobody is talking about how Johnson or the other three men died that night in Santa Rita. Callahan, other attorneys and the families of those victims that have families have asked for independent autopsies, but their requests have been denied. Indeed, as of this writing, the authorities have said very little, refusing even to acknowledge whether or not they have investigated the cause of death. Three of the bodies, including Johnson's remain in the County morgue. Friends and relatives of the men are pressuring the county to release the bodies so the men can be put to rest.

Peter finished the article. He thought Merrillee had done a good job. It was Mariah's idea to do the piece. Her friends in the mainstream press weren't willing to touch the story, so she called up Merrillee, who had worked with Mariah before. In addition, they had both dated the same man for several months until he told them both goodbye and moved to Hawaii with another woman neither Mariah or Merrillee had ever heard of. Mariah was convinced there was some kind of cover up going on over the deaths in the riot. She told Peter she could not recall another time when the bodies of the dead were kept for so long. Peter agreed but wondered what she could do about it. Mariah was working whatever angle she could. This news article was part of that crusade.

Peter sat outside Peet's off of North Shattuck. This part of town was completely gentrified. It had been heading sharply in that direction back in 1980. The transformation was now complete. There were still a few old hippies hanging out. That was probably due to the presence of the Hog Farm house over near Live Oak Park. You had to respect those Hog Farm folks, thought Peter. They never sold out. Plus, any cooptation they were involved in was on their terms, not the establishment's. He had run into Wavy Gravy once or twice since leaving Berkeley. He had also run into Southwester at a rock festival in Oregon. Other than that, he had had no contact with them. That was how it seemed to go. Even though he spent many nights on one of their couches or up on their Laytonville farm when he lived in the Bay Area, the actual contact just drifted away. Life in the fast lane or something. Still, he felt that he could run into any of the Farmers he used to know and pick up almost right where they had left off over twenty years ago. He also felt that way about Cat or even Nathaniel if he should be so lucky to run into either of them. He finished his coffee and headed toward the Rose Garden near Live Oak Park. He felt like getting high.

Mariah sat at the bar in Larry Blake's. Peter was meeting her there. She sipped on a glass of wine. Peter walked through the door. He walked over and sat on the stool next to her. She rubbed his thigh and they kissed. The bartender set a coaster in front of Peter.

"Anchor Steam, please," said Peter. He smiled at Mariah. His afternoon had been very relaxing. After smoking a pipe of very good weed in the Rose Garden, he sat on a bench for at least an hour watching people and birds. Then he went to the library and caught up on the Red Sox, the war in Iraq, and the world of rock and roll.

"How was your day? he asked her.

"Boring," she replied. "I spent the morning in court playing games with the prosecutor. I slept in my office this afternoon. No news on Porgy and no response to the article."

"Good article, by the way." Peter took a long draw from the beer that was set in front of him.

"I'm hoping I can get a mainstream outlet to run it," said Mariah. "I've got a call into Jasmin."

"We can ask Merrillee if we can send it out to various internet sites and blogs," said Peter. "That will spread it around. You'd be surprised how far and wide something like that can go."

"Good idea. I'm sure she'll tell us to go ahead." Mariah ordered another glass of wine. "Are you hungry? We can get something here."

"Sounds good to me." They ordered sandwiches. Peter asked for another beer.

A Week Later

Mariah's cell rang. She was on the Bay Bridge on her way to a lunch date with Jasmin. She answered.

"Hello? Mariah Callahan."

"Ms. Callahan?" The caller was a woman with a slight accent. She sounded Mexican. "My name is Esperanza Cruz. I am Porgy Johnson's oldest daughter, even though I only knew him as Esteban Cruz."

Mariah's heart jumped a beat. Finally. Maybe there would be a break in this case. "Hi. I'm in my car right now, but can I call you back in about ten minutes?"

"Sure." Esperanza hung up.

Mariah drove into San Francisco. She headed towards Embarcadero and looked for a place to park. Her luck was with her, as she found a spot in less than a minute. She locked up her car and began walking to the restaurant where she was meeting Jasmin. She dialed Esperanza back. The phone rang.

"Hi," said Mariah. "Thanks for waiting. Can I ask where you are?"

"Portland, Oregon." answered Esperanza.

"How did you hear about my connection to your father?" Mariah wondered.

"I saw the article by Merrillee Jackson on a website I check every once in a while," answered Esperanza. "I read it at least ten times before I was convinced it was about my father."

"Did you know he was in California?" Mariah really had no idea how well Porgy had kept in touch with his family.

"My mom mentioned that he might be in the States," said Esperanza. "When I talked with her in April last, she told me that he had stopped by her place in Oaxaca. I guess he stayed for a day or two and while he was there, Mom got a message that Dad's mom had died. Mom told me she told Dad not to go to the funeral, but she had a feeling he would."

Which turned out to be a fateful decision, thought Mariah.

"I would like to come down and meet you," said Esperanza. "I'm not doing much these days so I can come down whenever."

"Great. Give me a call when you get here. I can put you up while you're down here." Between her and Peter they could figure something out.

"I'll be on a flight tomorrow."

"Call me when you get your flight info," Said Mariah. "I'll try and meet you at the airport. It's better to come in to Oakland if you can."

"Thanks." Esperanza bit back her tears. "I wish I

had known he was in the States. I would have come and visited. He was a great dad when I was young, Ms. Callahan."

"I believe you." Esperanza hung up. Mariah put her cell back in her pocket. She saw Jasmin inside the restaurant and entered. The two women hugged each other in greeting.

As soon as Mariah sat down, a waitperson appeared. Both ordered iced tea and fajitas. "You won't believe this," said Mariah. "But my client's daughter just called."

"Is that who you were talking to?" asked Jasmin.

"Yeah. She read that article online and found my phone number." Mariah couldn't believe her luck. "I'm guessing my office gave her my cell once she identified herself."

"So," asked Jasmin. "Where does that put you?"

"I think it helps a lot." Mariah took a deep breath. "She can help us un-demonize her father. Especially if you can help us." A strategy was forming in Mariah's mind.

"How do you mean?" Jasmin was wary, but interested.

"Well, " began Mariah. "My interest in this is finding out how Porgy was killed. Peter is interested in rehabilitating his friend's name. Neither of us believes he killed that woman back in 1980. But whoever killed him in Santa Rita probably disagrees with our take on the situation. I think if we find out how he was killed we might find out who really did commit that murder back then. If his daughter is so inclined, her willingness to talk about her father might help people remember Porgy was human just like everyone else. I know it's reaching for something that probably doesn't exist, but that reminder might help someone else from back then remember something about that murder that they conveniently forgot out of fear or for some other reason."

"And?" Jasmin knew what was coming next. "I'm guessing you want me to help you in the media aspects of your little campaign."

"Yes." Mariah saw no reason to beat around the bush. "If you would."

"But what if you're wrong?" Jasmin asked. "I don't want to hitch my wagon to a lie. I mean, this is my career we're talking about here."

Mariah took an ice cube from her glass and chewed on it, crunching loudly. "It's my career too, Jasmin. I wouldn't be doing this if I didn't think I was right. You know me. Shit, even in high school I was always careful to only join stuff that I was convinced was right."

"Yeah, but this is closer to home than women's rights and the Democrats, Mariah," argued Jasmin. "The DAs and cops around here don't like the press turning over rocks and exposing their misdeeds and corruption."

Mariah looked disgusted. "Fuckin' media. You guys act like your job is to do PR for the authorities instead of keeping a close eye on them. What do they teach you all in journalism school these days?"

Jasmin pushed her chair back and stood up. "Don't tell me how to do my job, Mariah. Just 'cause we're old friends doesn't mean you have a right to dis me like that."

Mariah held back a smile. She knew Jasmin well enough that once you challenged her integrity she would do whatever it took to prove you wrong. "Sorry, Jasmin. I just get a little pissed off these days about shit like Fox-News and all the other networks mimicking them. Or Judith Miller and the *New York Times* printing every goddam lie that Cheney and Rumsfeld put out there to get us into these wars overseas."

"I'll be back," said Jasmin. Her face had a smile on it again. "I've gotta' pee."

Mariah finished her sandwich and waited. Jasmin was taking her time. The waitperson brought the check and Mariah gave him her Visa card. By the time he brought back the invoice Jasmin was sitting across from Mariah again.

"I don't know why or how you do it girl," she began. "I'll see what I can do. Don't tell me what your strategy is, though. If this guy's daughter is a good interview give me a call. Meanwhile, send me what you have for background. I read the article in that Hunter's Point paper. Nice work. If you can talk that retired cop into going on TV, let me know and I'll set something up with him."

Mariah leaned across the table and kissed Jasmin on the cheek. "I knew you'd come through, girl."

"We'll see what happens," said Jasmin. The two women hugged.

Peter was at his apartment. He was online using a laptop that Mariah lent him and borrowing someone's wireless connection from somewhere else in the apartment building. Tesla's theories at work. He still hoped to find moonshadow. If not her, then maybe Roger or Fats. The likelihood of finding any of these folks was remote, but one never knew in these days of the internet. Mariah had found his address that way. He had found Bonita and Arlo, so you never knew what might happen. He had googled the article by Merrillee earlier and saw that it was on at least fifteen websites. Most of them were websites that dealt with prisoners' issues, leftist blogs or indymedia sites, but any publicity was good.

He never had found out what happened to Fats and Roger. He guessed that they made it somewhere safe. If Fats took the money he had buried all over his yard in Marin those two could set up wherever and whatever they wanted. Peter's connection went out. He tried to reconnect a couple of times then gave up. It was too nice to stay inside, anyhow. He left the apartment and walked to the Berkeley Bowl supermarket. He felt like cooking a chicken. He called Mariah as he walked to the Bowl and invited her for dinner.

September 20, 2007

Esperanza was in Mariah's office. Jasmin and her sound man Nguyen were setting up some equipment. In these days of handheld digital cameras, the videorecording process was considerably simpler than it had been only fifteen years earlier when Jasmin began this line of work. Esperanza fussed a little with her hair, which was very long, very black and straight. She was a strikingly beautiful woman. She had her father's dark skin, but her eyes were blue. Her lips were full and her build was that of a slender twenty-four year old. Nguyen looked around. He couldn't help but marvel at the three beauties surrounding him as he worked.

Esperanza sat in front of the window in Mariah's office. The San Francisco Bay could be seen behind her. Jasmin sat in a comfortable chair diagonally across from Esperanza. Mariah sat off to the side out of the camera's view. Esperanza spoke three languages--English, Spanish and German--and Jasmin spoke English and Spanish. The interview would be conducted in English but the two women were currently talking in

Spanish. It was the first language of both.

Nguyen indicated he was ready. He sat over to the side next to Mariah, who remained in the room at Esperanza's request.

Jasmin began. She explained to Esperanza that she would edit in an introduction regarding the incident at Santa Rita and Porgy's trial.

"Hi Esperanza. When was the last time you saw your father?"

"About a year and a half ago. I was visiting my sister in Oaxaca at the small restaurant my mother owns and he stopped in."

"Did your father help raise you and your sister?"

"Oh yes. He was always there for us. He was the one who taught us to speak, read and write in English and Spanish. Our mom taught us German. He was pretty much the primary caregiver. Mama ran the restaurant. She owned it before she met my dad."

"Did they ever tell you how they met?"

"Sort of. Mama said that when dad left the States he headed to Oaxaca because a friend of his had contacts down there. The first or second night he was in Oaxaca he ran into those friends almost by accident. One of them was my mom. The morning after they met, my mom and her friend took my dad up to their farm in the mountains."

"When were you born?"

"About a year and a half after my mom and dad met."

"What was life like? Did you have visitors? "

"Yeah. I guess it was kind of a normal life for a German-American couple living in the mountains near Oaxaca. Mama had friends from Germany coming through. Dad knew a lot of Mexicans and Indians and my sister and I had our own friends from other farms and houses around the area."

"Did you always know your dad under his assumed name, Esteban Cruz?"

"Yeah. I guess I did, although my mom called him Porgy when she was being playful."

"Does that bother you that you never knew his real name?"

"I guess some people think it should, you know. But, to me, it doesn't change who he was. A name is just a name, you know. It's kind of like a flag. It only means as much as you want it to."

"Did your mom know him as Porgy Johnson?"

"My mom knew he was a fugitive. That's why she helped hide him. She believed in his innocence and his politics. I guess a lot of people had those kind of politics back then."

"Did you know he was in the United States?"

"No. The first I heard of it was when I read an article about his death in some online alternative newspaper from San Francisco."

"You mean the article in the *Hunter's Point Weekly?*"

"Yeah."

"Do your mother or sister know?"

"My dad's lawyer is trying to reach them to let them know."

"Now that you know about your father's past, does it change your opinion of him?"

"You know, Jasmin, I figured I would get asked this question. After thinking about it a long time, I can honestly say no. Why? Because I think the fact that he had to kill people in Vietnam to stay alive haunted him even when he was in Mexico and far from the United States and its actions. It does make me more curious about his past and has also caused me to reconsider some of my beliefs, but it hasn't changed my love for or my opinion of my dad."

"What exactly do you mean by the statement it has also caused me to reconsider some of my beliefs?"

"Well, you know, there were a lot of people who joined groups like the Black Panthers and even the NPLF back when my father did. I guess they really believed that they could change stuff. Heck, even nowadays I run into people like that. Down in Oaxaca there is a whole movement against the government and the global capitalism thing that is ruining communities in Latin America and the rest of the world. Up in Seattle they had those huge protests in 1999 I think. Always before I didn't think about them too much. I read about them and even talked about them, especially with my dad who always kept himself informed, but I never felt like I wanted to be part of it. Now, maybe I do."

"What do you hope to do here in the Bay Area?"

"I came down here because Mariah Callahan, my dad's lawyer, invited me. Mariah and some other people--one who was one of my dad's best friends back in those days--are trying to do two things. They want to discover the circumstances of his death in Santa Rita and they want to clear his name of that murder back in 1980."

"Thank you for your time, Esperanza."

Nguyen turned off the recorder. Jasmin smiled.

"You were great girl." Jasmin hugged Esperanza.

Now, thought Jasmin, I have to get it on the air.

October 1, 2007

Peter was on Telegraph Ave. Porgy had finally been cremated. His ashes were with Esperanza. Peter was talking with MaryBeth, a street vendor who sold jewelry. He was surprised to see her. She was one of the few who had stayed on the street since the 1970s. It was lunchtime. Peter went across the street to Blondie's and ordered four slices. When they were ready, he brought them back. MaryBeth turned a milk crate over and gestured for him to sit. As they ate the pizza and sipped on a couple beers MaryBeth kept in her cooler, she recounted her last twenty seven years. Mostly, it was the story of her children growing up and her lovers leaving. While he was listening Peter watched the people go by. MaryBeth was handing him another beer when he felt a large presence in front of her table. Both he and Mary-Beth looked up.

"Fats!" she shouted. Peter said nothing. He couldn't believe it. Fats was still a big guy. His hair was nonexistent, but his eyes were as blue as ever. MaryBeth was in front of the table hugging and kissing him. Peter guessed that Fats might have been one of those lovers. When the kissing was over, Fats looked over at Peter.

"Hey. Fancy meeting you here." They hugged.

"Yeah," smiled Peter. "The surprises keep coming."

MaryBeth had a couple of customers. They looked like suburbanites from the other side of the Hills. They were the type that kept the Telegraph Ave. street vendors in business. She asked them to wait a minute and looked at Peter and Fats. "Hey guys. I'll meet you at Larry Blake's in an hour."

"Sounds good." Fats hugged her. He and Peter headed to the next block and disappeared into Larry Blake's. The two men grabbed a booth near the back. Fats went up to the bar and ordered two beers and two shots of Maker's Mark. He came back to the booth with the shots. A waiter followed right after with the beers.

"Hey...," Peter started. Fats held up his hand. He handed a shot to Peter and took one himself. The two men tapped their shot glasses against each other and drank them back.

"So..." said Fats. "What are you doing here?

"And I could ask the same of you." Peter picked up his beer and drank.

"I've been living down in Oakland for about a year growing weed for a pot club."

"Medicinal stuff, huh?" Peter smiled.

"Yeah."

"Well, I came out here in May or so to help Porgy

get out of jail."

"Porgy? He's still around?" asked Fats.

"He's dead," said Peter. "Died in that riot out at Santa Rita."

"That fuckin' sucks." Fats shifted his weight in the booth. "I thought he was in Mexico."

"He was. Came back for his mom's funeral last winter and got popped in a traffic stop in Oakland. His sheet was hot since he was on *America's Most Wanted* a couple months earlier."

"Fuckin' police state." Fats looked down at the table.

"Anyhow, I've kind of fallen for his lawyer," continued Peter. "And we're trying to get his name cleared. Plus we want to find out how the hell he got killed. He didn't even know there was some kind of riot cooking up out there. When I saw him he was mostly concerned with how apolitical and pointless all the gang-banger shit was that he was running into in jail."

"Shit."

"Where you been?" asked Peter. "Last I heard your house burned down."

Fats laughed. "Oh yeah, that. Me and Roger took different modes of transportation to Hawaii. We hung there for about three years. Roger split and last I heard he was in Virginia running some computer-related company. He took all his dope money and put it into that. I stayed in Hawaii until last year. Then I ran into an old friend from the Haight who set me up in this medicinal marijuana growing thing. Remind me to give you some before I leave."

Peter smiled. He was getting low. "I've been trying to find moonshadow since I been out here. I figured she could verify this information Mariah--that's the lawyer who was working for Porgy--got from an old undercover cop who is convinced that Ra killed Rosie. Did you keep in touch with moonshadow's old boy-friend Ben?"

Fats rubbed his chin. Peter remembered he always did that before he had something to say that he didn't want to say. "I did keep in touch. In fact, I spoke with him about six months ago. He's in the music business now. moonshadow died of breast cancer about a year ago. I'm sorry."

Peter looked down. He felt tears coming. There was no shame in them. He never stopped loving her. Just so sad. He raised his glass. "To moonshadow, probably the best girlfriend I ever had."

Fats followed suit. They drank until the bar closed.

The following day Peter met Mariah at the Royal Cafe for breakfast. It hadn't changed much since Peter washed dishes there in 1977. They caught up over cof-fee. It had been a few days since they were together.

"I ran into Fats last night," began Peter.

"Was he the drug dealer guy you told me about that Rosie McNamara was going to see the night she was murdered.?"

"The very same."

"How did that go?" Mariah looked over the menu.

"Well," Peter took off his jacket. "I was hanging out on Telegraph talking with one of the street vendors I used to know when he appeared out of nowhere. We ended up going to Larry Blake's and drank until they closed."

"Wow."

"Yeah. He told me that moonshadow died last year from breast cancer."

"I'm so sorry, Peter." She reached across the table and touched his arm. He looked up. Then she moved her chair to the same side of the table as his and hugged him tightly.

"Thanks," said Peter. "Fats didn't have much else to say related to the case , though."

Late October 2007

The Red Sox won the Series earlier in the month. Iraq was still a killing field. Peter and Mariah were at the flea market again. He hoped to run into Rain. Esperanza accompanied them. She was still living at Mariah's. She was working in San Francisco at a restaurant off Market Street. She had contacted her mother after a week or two of frustration. The news of Porgy's death shook up her mother pretty bad. Esperanza told Mariah that they were still deeply in love with each other even though they had gone their separate ways. Her mom was considering coming to California.

Esperanza had spent the better part of the previous day reading Mariah's notes about her father's case. Earlier, she and Peter had spent a couple days at the library reading newspaper microfilm about the NPLF, SLA, and the Telegraph Avenue scene. She had to admit it was fascinating if only because it was so different from the world today.

Mariah and Esperanza stopped to buy some coffee. Peter walked on ahead then stopped to wait. Coffee purchased, the two women caught up.

"Why don't Esperanza and I go shopping?" suggested Mariah. "While you see if you can find Rain?"

"That makes sense," agreed Peter. "If you run into her, hold on to her. We can meet by the BART station at 2:00."

"Sounds good." Mariah gave Peter a quick hug. She and Esperanza headed down a row of stalls. Peter went in another direction. He was lost in thought when he heard someone call his name. It was Rain. She had a stall and was selling auto parts and tools. Peter stopped. Rain hugged him.

"Have a seat, man" she pulled out a wooden box and turned it over. Peter sat down. "You know, Peter, you look almost the same as you did twenty or whatever years ago."

Peter looked at Rain. Except for the fact she had no acne, she didn't look all that different either. "You do, too."

Rain pulled a cooler out of her car. "You want a beer?"

Peter took a bottle out of the ice. Rain handed him an opener. She took one for herself.

"Are you moving back out here, Peter?" asked Rain. Peter laughed.

"Well, I've been here since May. I guess I'm staying a while."

"You got money?"

"Yeah." Peter nodded. "I sold my house before I left the east coast. It's keeping me going."

"Cool."

"Plus I got a little bit of retirement money."

"One of them 401Ks?" asked Rain.

"Yeah. For whatever it's worth." Peter finished his beer. Rain handed him another. "I'm not real big on the Wall Street thing, you know."

"You could take a bunch of it out and grow pot," suggested Rain.

"I've thought of it, believe me."

A customer was looking at Rain's tool collection. It looked like he was considering buying a set of wrenches and some gauges. Rain stood up and talked with him. Peter watched folks walk by. He was hungry. He walked across the way and bought a couple breakfast burritos from a Latino guy opposite Rain's stall. By the time he returned to his seat on the box Rain had made her sale. He gave her one of the burritos.

"Thanks." She unwrapped it and began eating. Peter did the same.

"So where's that woman you were with? She's pretty cute." Rain had always liked both sides of the sexual divide.

"She's here somewhere." replied Peter.

Rain had another customer.

When she finished with the transaction and sat back down, Peter asked. "Do you remember how I was asking you about Nathaniel?"

"Yeah..."

"Well, the reason I asked is because I'm hoping to run into him or Cat or both." He explained.

"Why?" asked Rain.

"You know that riot out in Santa Rita a little while back?"

"Yeah...?"

"Well, a friend died in it."

"Who?"

"Do you remember Porgy?" asked Peter.

"He was a black guy, right? Kind of tall and thin with a small afro most of the time? Pretty laid back. Cute."

"Yeah. That 's the guy."

"It was him?" shouted Rain. "I thought he split to Mexico way back when that narc woman got killed. You know the one who was with those SLA kind of people." Peter motioned to Rain to be quieter.

"Oops, sorry." She continued, whispering. "So what do Nathaniel or Cat have to do with this?"

"Well, to make a long story short," answered Peter. "I don't know. Cat was always convinced that another dude in the house where Porgy and Rosie lived was the killer--"

"You mean that kind of sleazy guy Ra?" asked Rain. "Didn't you have a girlfriend who lived there?

"Yeah," Peter replied. "moonshadow."

"That Ra guy always was kind of a prick," thought

Rain out loud. "But I ain't seen him in years. I think he dealt crack for a while."

"Well, he was a narc, too," said Peter. "And the reason I came out here in May was to help Porgy get free. You were right. He was gone for a long time but then he came back for his mom's funeral and got busted partly because he was on *America's Most Wanted* and partly because he was riding around with some dumb fuckers. The cops stopped the car and he got taken in. Now he's dead. I still want to clear his name and find out how he died in that riot."

"Shit," said Rain.

"So that woman I was with was Porgy's lawyer and she contacted me to see if I knew anything." Peter continued. "I came out and got a place. Now me and her are kind of seeing each other so I have a greater reason to stay for a while."

Rain nodded. "I haven't seen Cat in about ten years. The last time I saw her she was pretty fucked up on some kind of pharmaceuticals. She started screaming at me and then she passed out. I called 911 and split. Nathaniel lives in Albany at some kind of group house. He's free to come and go, but he mostly stays in. I can give you the address."

"Thanks, Rain." Peter handed her a piece of paper and a pen. She wrote down the information. Rain took two more beers from the cooler and they relaxed. Peter's cell rang just as he finished his beer. It was Mariah.

"Keep in touch, Rain."

"I'm here almost every Saturday, Peter." She stood up and kissed his cheek. He responded in kind and left.

Two Days Later

Peter was on the San Pablo bus going north. He hoped to find Nathaniel at home. He had called Rain for his number but she didn't have one. He got off the bus at San Pablo and Marin and headed west. The house was on Evelyn Avenue somewhere. Peter was in no hurry. He had no idea what to expect and merely hoped to make contact with Nathaniel. When he got to the cross street he turned right and looked for the address. It was four blocks south of Solano. A nondescript California house. One level stucco building. Cacti in the front yard. He went up the walk and rang the bell. After two rings a woman answered the door. Mid-forties with short black hair. She looked at him questioningly.

"Hi," began Peter. Is Nathaniel around?"

"The woman shook her head. "He's out shopping."

"Can I come back later?" asked Peter.

"He might stay at his girlfriend's." The woman seemed nervous and looked like she wanted to close the door in Peter's face but was too polite.

Peter took out a piece of paper with his phone number on it. He handed it to the woman at the door. "Can you please make sure he gets this?" asked Peter. "I'm a friend of his from a long time ago."

"Sure, I can do that." She closed the door. Peter turned and left.

November 1, 2007

Dia de los Muertos. Mariah and Esperanza were sitting in Mariah's living room. The two of them had just woke up. They were waiting for Peter to bring them breakfast. Mariah was reviewing the aspects of the impending suit against the prison, county and state authorities regarding Porgy's death. Progress had been slow. She had some transcripts from the sheriff's department that detailed the quelling of the riot. Nothing she had read seemed too relevant to Porgy or two of the other men killed. It seemed to Mariah and the lawyers working for the families of the other fatalities that Porgy and two of the other men died in the same part of the prison around the same time. All three had been in the visitors' room just prior to the lockdown. However, nothing had been said or provided that revealed what part of the prison the deaths occurred.

"I want to get access to the surveillance films from the prison that night. Especially any that feature where Porgy was. I doubt that he was returned to his cell. It would have taken too much time."

"Can you get them?" asked Esperanza.

"I don't know," answered Mariah. "I think it's a legitimate request but I don't know if the state will think so. I mean, I think it ties in with the investigation into the circumstances of your father's death, but the state might say that it doesn't."

"But why?"

"Because they don't want us to see something that either they did or prevented the prisoners from doing."

"But why?" Esperanza's occasional naivete pissed Mariah off. To her credit she was learning fast.

"Because they wanted the prisoners to die, Esperanza!" said Mariah. "That's why."

The women heard a knock on the door. Mariah got up and opened it. Peter stood there. He had some coffees and croissants "Hi ladies." He smiled.

Both women seemed grateful for his appearance. Mariah knew she shouldn't get mad at Esperanza. After all, her upbringing seemed to have sheltered her from the harsh realities of twenty-first century life in the capitalist uberworld. It's not like Oaxaca was pretty and nothing bad happened, but Porgy and his partner certainly seemed to have done their best to keep their children unaware of how cruel some humans and their systems could be. Peter sat down and began distributing the goodies. The three of them decided to spend the day in the Mission partaking in the day's festivities.

November 10, 2007

Mariah's cell buzzed. It was the second Saturday in November. Early morning. She looked at her phone. A text from Jasmin.

"I finally got the show on. Tonight at 6:30. Esperanza's interview in full."

Esperanza had just left for work. Mariah forwarded the text message to her and Peter. That evening the three of them met at Peter's. Chinese take-out at 6:00 PM. The television on.

The show had a newsmagazine format. Jasmin's story on Porgy was the second of three. She had ten minutes. After a very brief introduction that began with a brief description of the Santa Rita riot, she told the viewers about Porgy's past. Military brat, draftee, Cambodian invasion, Black Panther, Telegraph Ave. denizen, NPLF member, suspected murderer, and fugitive. *America's Most Wanted* feature, inmate and casualty of riot, cause of death unknown. She mentioned that his lawyer was working with other lawyers representing the riot's fatalities trying to discover the cause of death and get some kind of settlement. She also told the audience that some of Porgy's friends and family members were trying to clear his name. Then came the interview.

Dick Stevens watched the program from his hospital room. His cancer and emphysema had worsened considerably the past month. He was surprised that he hadn't heard about Johnson's death via the grapevine that cops working and retired maintained. He guessed that people who knew about his interest and connection to the case didn't want to bother him given his medical situation. Ra had been haunting his dreams the past couple nights. Dreams of when he first met him. Stevens had made the mistake of thinking he was a brother with the same motivations as himself. Justice and a belief in the American system. Even though Stevens got called a Tom a lot of the time, even by friends and family, he believed in his job and the system. It soon became clear that Ra was not a like-minded soul. He was only in it for himself. Didn't give a shit about nobody. After watching the show, Stevens told himself that if he made it through this latest bout in the hospital he would try and help that lawyer again.

November 11, 2007

Nathaniel had always been on the thin side. Now he was even more so. Peter wondered at first if he might have AIDS. The bout with crack must have aged him a lot. Even though he was only 60, he looked like he was 80. Very little hair and many wrinkles. His eyes still sparkled blue, though. Peter asked him if he still smoked weed. Nathaniel said he had a prescription for it and took out his stash. They did a couple bong hits. Peter listened to the birds in a tree outside Nathaniel's window. Nathaniel refilled the bowl on the bong and handed it to Peter. Peter took another toke. Medicinal weed tended to be very strong. This stuff was fantastically so. It would take a few minutes before Peter could get his thoughts straight again.

"So, how did you find out where I was?" asked Nathaniel. He filled the bowl again and took a hit.

"I ran into Rain at the flea market," answered Peter. "I was asking about you and some other folks from the old days. She told me where you lived."

"Did she tell you about what I've been up to?"

Nathaniel sounded a bit wary.

"Not really," said Peter. "Just that your health had failed some."

"Yeah." Nathaniel looked at his fingers and opened and closed his fist. "Fuckin' crack did me in."

"Crack, huh." Peter looked out the window. Two birds were chasing each other in and out of the tree. "I never figured you for that shit. You always stayed away from the hard stuff."

"I know," agreed Nathaniel. "Somehow it hooked me, though."

"Happened to a lot of good people." Peter wanted to change the subject but wasn't sure what he wanted to change it to. He wasn't in the mood to listen to somebody regret their past.

"So," It was like Nathaniel sensed Peter's thought. "Why are you in the Bay Area, man? I didn't think I'd ever see you again. We used to have some good times."

Peter told Nathaniel the story of Mariah's letter, Porgy's bust and everything else that had followed the letter. He was to the part about the riot when Nathaniel interrupted him.

"I saw that interview on TV last night," He said. "I know about Porgy dying. Too bad. He wasn't a bad guy. Plus, he got screwed by the cops for that female narc's murder."

"Yeah. I think he did, too."

"No." Nathaniel leaned forward. "I know he did."

Peter looked at Nathaniel. What was he trying to say?

Nathaniel looked around, as if he was afraid some-one else was in the room. He scratched his elbows and ran his hand over his bald head. "I used to buy my crack from that dude Ra."

Peter did not react. "Yeah?"

"No. Seriously." Nathaniel sat back again. "Me and some other crackheads were squatting in this aban-doned warehouse near Pardee Street. Do you know where that is?"

Peter nodded. One of the warehouses on Pardee had been the scene of some pretty famous afterhours parties the last time he lived in the Bay Area. Peter had seen sev-eral punk bands in their early incarnations at those par-ties. He'd also been dosed with some of the best LSD he'd ever eaten at various post-Grateful Dead show bashes there.

"Well. " continued Nathaniel. "That dude Ra used to come around every couple days with a half ounce of rock. We would sell half of it and smoke the rest. He was giving it to this one chick there for sex. She wasn't a crack whore 'cause Ra was her only trick. It was kind of a twisted love thing."

"You sure it was Ra?" asked Peter.

"Yeah, definitely," insisted Nathaniel. "He wasn't going by that name--he called himself Blue--but I know it was Ra."

"How can you be sure?"

"Peter, man." Nathaniel stood up and walked around his small room. He turned up the radio. Dylan's "Love-sick" was playing. "I used to sleep with that girl Rhiannon at the NPLF house. I saw Ra almost every day for about six months when me and her were fucking each other. I know it was Ra."

Peter nodded. Nathaniel's certainty was convincing.

"He got shot in Oakland."

"Who?" asked Peter. "Ra?"

"Yeah," answered Nathaniel. "He owed some dude a bunch of money. Seems he started smoking the product and got into debt. So some gangbanger had him killed. He never came back even though we owed him money. I heard the body was dumped in the estuary. It floated up somewhere near where all those fishing boats are. The newspapers never said much about it, but we heard about it when some other guy started bringing us the rock. I got busted a few months later and did two years at Folsom."

"Bummer. Folsom, huh?"

"Actually," said Nathaniel thoughtfully. "It was probably the best thing that could have happened to me. I kicked crack, met some glass blower guy who was doing two for trafficking who taught me how to blow glass when he got out. Now I make dishes and other stuff that certain rich people like to pay too much for."

Peter looked around the room. There were a good number of very beautiful glassware pieces on the bookshelf and the bay window sill. "Wow. Do you have shows and stuff?"

"Some woman who runs a gallery in Port Richmond sponsored a glass show a couple months ago," said Nathaniel. "There were several blowers but I was the featured artist. Of course, her and I were sleeping together then."

Peter smiled. Nathaniel still had a way with the women apparently. Even despite his almost wraith-like appearance. "That reminds me, Nathaniel. Whatever happened to Juno?"

Juno was a college student studying archeology who fell in love with Nathaniel, quit college, moved into a schoolbus and eventually ended up sleeping with Peter after Nathaniel grew tired of her.

"She went back to St. Louis and married her boyfriend from college," answered Nathaniel. "Last I heard she was working on a Mayan dig deep in Mexico. Her husband is her assistant. She calls me about once every eighteen months."

"Good for her." Peter filled the bong and lit the weed in the bowl. The two men spent a couple more hours together reminiscing.

Peter was at Civic Center Plaza. He was heading to the San Francisco library hoping he could find some microfilm of the old San Francisco underground newspapers. There was some Christian End Times convention going on at the Moscone Center. Bunch of crazy apocalyptic Christians whose kids called themselves Jesus' Army. Ready to kill for Christ. Wasn't that a Fugs song? Two pretty young women with blonde hair walked alongside Peter and handed him some literature. Anti-gay, anti Muslim, pro-Bush.... The apostles of hate representing the prophet of love?

He saw Esperanza arguing with two young men who were handing out the same literature. He waved across the Plaza. She used his greeting as an excuse to walk away from the disciples. They followed her until they saw Peter. Then they asked him if he was interested. Peter waved the leaflet he had been handed and the two young men walked away, looking for another bystander to proselytize. Esperanza waited on a nearby bench.

"Hey, Peter." she looked up at him. "How you doing?"

"All right. You ready to read microfilm?"

"Yeah," answered Esperanza. "What are we looking for exactly?"

"I don't know." Peter sat down. "I guess anything about the NPLF, your dad, Thomas Africa, or Ra."

They got up and walked towards the library. Once inside, they procured several reels of microfilm, made change, and found two microfilm machines next to each other. Most of the rolls were from the underground newspaper collection, but they had also obtained some from the *Bay Guardian, East Bay Express, Oakland Tribune,* and the *Berkeley Gazette.* Esperanza had barely loaded her roll when she whispered to Peter.

"Hey! Here's a picture of my dad. Man does he look young." Peter moved his chair next to Esperanza's to get a better look. Sure enough, it was Porgy. The picture was taken during a rally against the Bakke decision on Sproul Plaza. Porgy was on the stage waiting his turn to speak. Peter recalled the day. The decision itself was essentially racist, yet used the language of anti-discrimination to claim that Bakke had been denied entrance into UC Medical School because he was white. The courts agreed with him, despite the historical evidence that non-whites had been denied entrance because they weren't white for decades. Then again, there was the fact that Bakke wasn't as qualified as many of the non-white applicants who did get into the school. Perhaps the worst aspect of the case was that it gave vocalization to the white-man-as-victim mentality that right wing ideologues and radio hosts turned into a booming business and a dangerous political movement. Porgy gave a great speech that afternoon. Then a crowd of frat boys attacked him. Porgy got away after several street people--black and white--chased the frat boys away. It wasn't that the street people cared too much about the politics. It was because Porgy was considered a brother, while frat boys were the enemy.

"Seeing him so young. My dad was pretty good looking," thought Esperanza aloud.

"The women sure thought so," agreed Peter. "And probably a few men did, too."

Esperanza giggled. She copied the photo of her father and continued looking for more articles and pictures that mentioned him. Peter followed suit. Three hours later they left the library with close to a hundred photocopies. Most of the articles were about the NPLF, the firebombing of the Berkeley police cars and Porgy's indictment and disappearance. Peter was hungry.

"You want to get something to eat?" he asked Esperanza.

"Yeah. Chinatown's pretty close. Let's go." They headed to Kearny Street, found a small place down some steps and went in. Peter ordered two TsingTaos. When the waiter came back with the beers, Esperanza told him the rest of the order.

"So, Peter," Esperanza sipped her beer. "What was my dad's life like when you all hung out?"

"I met him in 1976 not long after I got to Berkeley with my girlfriend at the time. He showed us around and introduced us to some folks," began Peter. "We used to drink pitchers of beer with him at this pizza joint on the north side of Berkeley. Pitchers were a buck and we would spend an afternoon drinking. It was usually on a Friday 'cause that's when I got my unemployment check. He was a charmer with the women, but didn't really take advantage of them, at least not according to the terms we all understood back then. The cops didn't like him but left him alone unless they could catch him with a lit joint or an open bottle, which wasn't very often. He slept wherever he laid his head. Didn't have a real address until he moved in with the NPLF."

"Did he drink a lot?"

"We all did," answered Peter. "Got high a lot, too. It's just how it was." Peter motioned for two more Tsing-Taos. He looked back to Esperanza. "I never saw or heard of your dad doing anything to hurt anyone. Whatever he saw and did in Vietnam and Cambodia must have convinced him that nothing was worth hurting people. He told me once when we were at a friend's place doing some acid that even though he sometimes felt like killing the cops, he knew that he could never plan such an act. He was a good dude. I sometimes feel like we didn't do enough to get the charges dropped, but at the time there was no way the law was ever gonna' believe anything but that Porgy killed that woman. If we didn't disappear like we did the law would have found a way to put us all away. If you want an idea of how it was, think of how it was was here for Arabs and Pakistanis after 911. The truth didn't fuckin' matter. It was payback time."

Peter's monologue was interrupted by the waiter setting the beers and some bowls of soup on the table. Both he and Esperanza ate it quickly. The rest of the food appeared. They continued to eat.

"How did you get him out of the States?" asked Esperanza.

"It was actually pretty easy," answered Peter. He recalled the last phone call he had with Porgy. "He was staying in Kansas City, Missouri. Crashing on people's couches. Mostly it was old friends of his from the neighborhood he grew up in out there. Things got hot after the FBI put him on their list. I arranged a ride for him to Tucson. While he was there he stayed with an ally of the movement, shall we say. I arranged a fake passport and birth certificate for him. I sent that to Tucson. Porgy was given five hundred dollars, most of it in Mexican pesos, and a ride to Nogales. He walked across the border there and took buses to Oaxaca. I was told via our Tucson contact that he met the people he was supposed to meet. One of them turned out to be your mother, apparently."

"And the rest is history," laughed Esperanza.

"Yeah," Peter smiled. They finished the meal and headed toward the BART station. Both were going to Mariah's place.

Peter enjoyed hanging out with Esperanza. She reminded him of his daughter. Esperanza was chronologically probably a couple years older, but she shared an exuberance and intelligent naivete with Peter's girl, Leda.

December 20th, 2007

Mariah was happy. She was on her way to obtain copies of the surveillance video from Santa Rita the day and night of the riot. The threat of a suit had convinced the DA to release the material to her and the two other attorneys. She hoped the video would be complete. If not, she hoped it would at least show what happened in the area Porgy was in before, during and after he died. The office she was heading to had copied all of the video onto DVD-Rs and cataloged them. It looked like she would be watching lots of video over the next day. She hoped to get Peter and Esperanza to join her. That would help ensure that nothing was missed.

Then, if there was something there that showed Porgy's death occurring under what were at the least questionable circumstances, Mariah might have a genuine case. Whether or not she could convince the DA to file criminal charges was a big question. A civil suit seemed more likely. Although the wrongful death suit interested Peter and Esperanza, their real interest was in clearing Porgy's name of the murder of McNamara.

She parked her car in a space reserved for attorneys and headed into the building. After a half hour of searches and waiting for prosecutors and their assistants, then a ten-minute conversation with the Assistant DA for the county, Mariah was in the building's elevator with a padded envelope containing several DVD-Rs. Before she left the building she placed them in her shoulder bag. Found her car, got in and headed to her apartment.

Peter had spent the night. He and Esperanza were drinking coffee and listening to some corridas mix that Esperanza liked. Mariah unlocked her door and said hello. Both replied in kind.

"It's time to watch some video," said Mariah. She opened her bag, took out the envelope and handed it to Peter. He figured out the sequential order and placed the first disc into the DVD player. It was marked with the date of Mariah's last visit with Porgy and the time of 1600 hrs. After a moment or two of gray on the television screen, a view of one of the prison yards came into view. Several men were milling around. A group of seven or eight seemed to be facing off with each other. Within ten minutes this group was fighting amongst themselves. Soon, several other prisoners were involved. Guards soon waded into the fray, beating men with clubs, while other guards appeared around the perimeter with what appeared to be tear gas guns. Soon, the yard was filled with gas clouds. This entire filming was fifty-eight minutes.

A series of numbers flowed across the screen. The same date appeared. The time was 1835 hrs. Then, once again the gray screen. The view from one camera focused on a corridor that was completely caged. Several men--seven to nine it seemed--were in the corridor cuffed and shackled to each other. A guard with a shotgun could be seen at the far end of the corridor on the other side of the cage. Another view, probably from another camera focused on the men's torsos and heads. Esperanza and Peter both let out a yelp at the same time. "Stop!" Mariah pushed the pause button on the remote. Peter stood up, walked over to the television and pointed at one of the shackled men.

"That looks like Porgy," he said. Mariah looked closer.

"It is," she agreed. "That means we need to find all of the videos that have this camera's view. Then maybe we can find out what happened."

Peter took out his cell to order some takeout from the Mexican place two blocks away. Mariah went into her bedroom to change into some jeans and a t-shirt. Esperanza pressed the play button on the remote and continued watching the video. It was fairly hi-quality. The cameras they had in the prison must have been digital. Despite the shadows one could make out many of the faces on both the uniformed men and the prisoners. The view she was watching was from some place high up. The lens was pointing into the yard and showed dozens of heavily armed law enforcement types wearing storm trooper uniforms like the ones in the *Star Wars* movies. She could hear shouting and a loudspeaker telling inmates to return to their cells. The armed men began to move towards a building. They were firing tear gas and some other kind of weapons that looked like they were shooting plastic bullets or some kind of little balls. The speakers were filled with popping sounds and the explosions of the grenades. The screen was filled with clouds. Peter finished placing the food order. The cloudy scene on the screen reminded him of the dry ice displays familiar to certain rock concerts.

"I'm walking down to get the food," he told Esperanza. "You want to come?"

Esperanza shook her head. "No." Peter walked out the door and closed it behind him.

Peter and Mariah were in bed. They had stopped watching the video an hour or so earlier. Esperanza was still watching and taking notes. They had yet to come to a place that showed what happened to Porgy and the rest of the men in the corridor. Mariah leaned into Peter. He felt her breasts against him underneath her t-shirt and began caressing them. She leaned into him more and kissed his neck and face. Peter turned towards her and they began kissing in earnest. She pulled her shirt over her head and pulled off her un-

derwear. Peter did the same. They threw back the cov-
ers and gave in to their desires.

The next morning they woke up entwined in each
other and the sheets.

January 4, 2008

The holidays were over. Esperanza had insisted on celebrating Christmas, so Peter and Mariah obliged. They decorated a small tree at Mariah's place, traded a couple gifts and went to Marin for dinner with Mariah's father and other relatives. New Year's Eve found the three of them at a blues club on Mason in San Francisco where they met up with Jasmin. Peter and Mariah spent part of New Year's Day with Michael and his son at a party at Michael's place in the Oakland Hills. Good food and liquor. Arlo and Bonita were also there. The ex-cop Stevens had called Mariah on January 3rd. He was out of the hospital and in a hospice in Emeryville. His prognosis was not too good. Six months to a year was the latest time span given to him. He wanted to talk over what Mariah had discovered since he went into the hospital. Mariah was hoping that he would be willing and able to speak with Jasmin, who seemed to be more interested in the case than before. Apparently, the segment that the station had run earlier was getting raves and notice for her.

Esperanza was at work. Mariah was on her way to meet with Stevens. Peter decided to watch more video from the prison. They had found most of the footage that showed the corridor where Porgy had been shackled with the others. However, they had not found any film that showed how the men died. Peter had to admit that watching the raw footage of the riot was fascinating on its own. Especially since the camera was merely mounted some place and had no agenda of its own. One saw everything in front of the lens without comment. Cinema verité.

Mariah parked her car in the hospice parking lot. She took her recorder and placed it in her bag. She grabbed a bag of fruit and some other food items that Stevens had asked for and went inside. The receptionist was very pleasant and showed her the way to Stevens' private room. The fact that it was private would make the conversation easier, thought Mariah. The door was open. Stevens was sitting up in his bed.

"Hi, Mr. Stevens," said Mariah. She set the bag of food on a tray next to his bed. He smiled and nodded hello. Mariah was surprised at how strong he looked. She expected much worse. He was a bit thinner than she remembered but his eyes were alive and his smile was real. She sat down and took out the recording device.

"Do you mind?" she asked, pointing at the recorder.

"Nah," said Stevens. "That's fine." Mariah offered

him a banana from the bag of food. He peeled it and began eating. "Thanks. Not much fresh fruit in this place."

"Let me tell you about where we are," began Mariah. "We got the interview with Porgy's daughter on television--"

"I saw that," interrupted Stevens. "Very attractive young woman. Well-spoken."

"Yeah," agreed Mariah. "Helped our cause, I think."

"So. What has the DA done?" asked Stevens. "Did you get the video from the riot? How about any testimony corroborating my take on Freedman or Ra as he called himself? "

Mariah smiled. It was good to see Stevens so ani-mated. "Well, we have some corroboration of your story regarding Ra. An old friend of Peter's and Porgy's told us that he used to sell crack for Ra in the 1980s. Apparently, Ra started smoking crack himself and ended up owing a good deal of money. This gen-tleman told us that Ra was killed and his body was found floating in the estuary. If positive ID exists of the corpse we haven't found it yet. Perhaps your con-tacts could help us there."

Stevens leaned forward. "Hold up." He pointed at the bureau across from his bed. "Can you reach into the top drawer and pull out the big envelope there?'

Mariah did so. She handed the envelope to Stevens. He reached in and pulled out some papers. He leafed through them, found what he was looking for and handed it to Mariah. It was a photocopy of a police report dated April 23, 1988. Mariah scanned the text.

Scene: Body reported by (name deleted), a fisherman operating out of the Oakland Estuary. Officers arrived at scene at 7:00 AM. Spoke to witness and walked over to body. Black male approximately 6 feet tall. 200 lbs. Body in early stages of decomposition. Probably delayed because of salt water. Coroner's unit arrived approximately 7:30 AM. Removed body.

Witness statement: (Name deleted) told officers he arrived at his boat around 3:30 AM morning of April 23, 1988. Worked on boat and fishing equipment until app. 5:30 AM. Went to breakfast at diner near estuary. Returned to boat app. 6:30 AM. Was getting ready to go into bay to fish when he decided to relieve himself in estuary. Walked thirty feet away from his boat along water and begin to urinate. Noticed body at this time. Went back to boat, moved it into position near body so that body would be lodged between boat and side of estuary. Called police on radio around 6:50 AM.

Mariah continued to scan the document. Most of the remaining text in the crime scene report was irrelevant as far as she was concerned. Officer's impressions, names, and so on. She looked at the next set of papers stapled together. They read "INTERNAL DOCUMENTS ONLY" across the top. Stevens yanked the set away and leafed through them until he found what he wanted to show her. Mariah read where his finger pointed.

> *Body has been identified as that of Ronnie Freedman of Los Angeles and Oakland, CA. Freedman worked as an informant for OPD, CHP and occasionally for various federal investigative agencies. In recent years he has been working as a narcotics informant in the Oakland crack cocaine scene. Cause of death is a gunshot entering the back of the head. .22 caliber weapon of delivery. THIS INFORMATION IS NOT TO BE RELEASED. CORPSE WILL REMAIN UNIDENTIFIED TO PRESS AND PUBLIC.*

Mariah re-read the text. This was almost a smoking gun. But could she do anything with it? Stevens was leaning back on his pillow. He had a smile on his face.

"How did you get this?" asked Mariah. Stevens put up his hand and waved it back and forth.

"You can't ask me that," he told her.

"Can I get copies?" asked Mariah. This stuff could be gold.

"If they have a copier here that you can use," answered Stevens. He wasn't going to let this stuff out of his sight. Mariah nodded. She took the two documents to the front desk and asked if there was a copier she could use. The receptionist brought her back into the manager's office and Mariah made the copies she needed. She returned the materials to Stevens. He put them back in the envelope and asked Mariah to place them back in the bureau. After she did so, they watched television for about thirty minutes. By then, Stevens was asleep. Mariah left a note asking him to call her and left.

She got on San Pablo Avenue and headed south towards her apartment. She was glad to have proof of Ra's existence and death. However, she still had nothing to link him to the murder of McNamara. The web of circumstance was growing tighter. She called Peter on her cell and asked him to meet her for lunch.

January 11th, 2008

Jasmin was at Mariah's place. Mariah had shown her the photocopied documents she got from Stevens. They were trying to reach Stevens to arrange an interview. He and Mariah had talked once since the fourth and he seemed stable. Now, however, Mariah was being told that Stevens' health had taken a bad turn and he was not allowed visitors. Meanwhile, Esperanza had located footage on the DVD-Rs that seemed to show Porgy's cause of death. The camera focused on the corridor where he and the other men were shackled showed a tear gas grenade hitting one of the cagelike walls with great force. Then another. They appeared to have been fired from the end of the corridor nearest the visitors room. After the second firing, the corridor filled with gas. The video showed Porgy and most of the other men gasping for breath. It then showed Porgy bending over and appearing to dry heave. After three minutes of this the sound of another explosion and the infusion of even more gas into the corridor was shown. Porgy then fell suddenly to the ground, pulling down most of the other men he was shackled to. A voice is heard yelling at the men to stand up. The officer at the other end of the caged-in corridor is shown with a gas mask on. He pointed his gun at the men in the corridor. The prisoners can be heard gasping for air and pleading with the guards and other lawmen to get them out of the cage. Fifteen minutes passed. Most of the men were still on the floor of the cage. Finally, the officer in view of the camera unlocked the gate at his end. He walked into the corridor and prodded the men on the ground with his gun. All but three of them managed to stand. Those that remained on the ground were prodded with the gun once more. Audio of one of the prisoners shouting--"You killed him you motherfucker.' The guard then hit that prisoner with the butt of his gun and knocked him on the floor. Two more officers appeared and kick the prisoners who are down. Another explosion and the camera went dead. After viewing this segment repeatedly, Peter and Mariah guessed that the last explosion was the sound of a guard shooting out the camera's lens.

Esperanza was quite upset. As far as she was concerned, her father was murdered in cold blood. After drinking herself to sleep the night after she first viewed this footage, she called her mother in Mexico and urged her to come up. Her mom was non-committal. She was afraid there might be legal problems if she did.

"So," began Jasmin after viewing the prison footage. "Should we talk about this on the segment or stick to the question of clearing Porgy's name?"

"Can we do both?" asked Esperanza. She was back from work and sitting with Mariah and Jasmin.

"It would be better to focus on the story that is most complete," answered Jasmin. "The problem is, though, that I'm not sure which one that is."

"It kind of depends on whether or not you can interview Mr. Stevens," interjected Mariah. "If you can't, then the prison riot seems to me to be the one to cover now."

Jasmin agreed. She took the disc that contained the footage of Porgy's death and placed it back in the player. She needed to study it more closely.

A Week Later

The hospice was trying to contact Mariah. They had called Peter's cell. She was in court. He left a message. Esperanza's mom was not going to come to California. There was an old problem with her passport and she didn't want to risk losing her residency status in Mexico because of some bullshit post-911 law made in Washington, DC. Esperanza understood. Her few months in the States had convinced her that there really were forces at work that didn't like people like her father, mother or herself. Peter was in San Francisco meeting with some folks involved in the San Francisco 8 defense committee.

Earlier, Peter had asked the lawyers he met at Arlo and Bonita's if the SF 8 group might be interested in taking up Porgy's case. The response had not been negative, but it was clear to Porgy that the interest was minimal. He was willing to attribute it to the fact that the San Francisco 8 defense was overwhelmed given their small numbers and the task facing them. There was a part of him, however, that wondered if there might be another reason--something regarding the politics of the NPLF and their disputes with many other leftist groups during their existence. Although it was all rather silly to Peter, he knew that arcane political disagreements were often the cause of irreparable fissures on the Left. Either way, they were meeting with him now. The group was willing to lend its support to the call for an investigation into the deaths at Santa Rita. Peter had found somebody to copy the DVD-Rs and was providing members of the SF 8 defense committee working with Peter, Mariah, Esperanza and the friends and families of the other men killed with those copies. The San Francisco 8, meanwhile, had finally been released from prison to await trial. Except, of course, for those men in prison because of other Panther-related convictions. Evidence hearings and other procedural bullshit was taking up a good deal of the released men's time.

Mariah left court. She checked her messages. Besides Peter's there was a call from Jasmin asking if she had arranged an interview with Stevens. There was also a short message from Esperanza regarding dinner. Mariah called Peter.

"Hey." Peter was on his way to the Civic Center BART Station.

"Hi, Peter." Mariah started her car. She was heading straight to Emeryville and the hospice. "Any clue as to what the hospice wanted?" She feared the worst. Part of

the reason she had not arranged an interview was because of Stevens' recent health. A slight cold had in-
fected his lungs. His doctor wanted him to go back into
the hospital, but he refused. It cost too much, he said.
Why waste money to keep a dying old man alive for
three more months? Mariah had her reasons, but Stevens wasn't interested.

"No. But it can't be good." Peter was at the top of
the elevator going into the station. "I'm getting on the
BART. See ya' later."

"I'll meet you at your place, love," said Mariah. She
closed her phone and drove north.

Pulling into the hospice parking lot, she saw an
ambulance. A stretcher bearing a person was being
placed in it. She parked quickly, got out and went
quickly over to the ambulance. It wasn't Stevens. She
went inside. The receptionist looked up.

"Hi. Ms. Callahan." her face expressed zero emo-
tion. Must be part of the training, thought Mariah.

"Hi. You guys called me earlier...."

"Yes," answered the receptionist. "Mr. Stevens
asked us to let you know that he went to the hospital.
He said you would want to know and that he had no
one else to tell."

"Which hospital?" asked Mariah.

"Alta Bates," answered the receptionist. "That's
where his doctor is today."

"Can I go to his room for a minute? In case there's
something he needs?"

"Well...," the receptionist hesitated. "The people who took him to the hospital were police officers. They asked me not to let anyone into his room."

Mariah tried not to bristle. She needed to get the documents in that bureau. "I've kind of been like his daughter since he got sick..," began Mariah. "Maybe there's something he really wants with him. I won't be long."

The receptionist looked around. There were no supervisors around. They were either on lunch or out in the parking lot with the ambulance. "Go quick," she whispered. She slipped Mariah the key. Five minutes later, Mariah was back. The papers were no longer in the room. She thanked the receptionist, pointed at her bag as if she had something from the room stashed in it and said goodbye. Alta Bates hospital was her next stop. Ten minutes later she was pulling into a visitors' parking lot. Not long after that she was outside Stevens' room. Two Oakland Police Department uniformed police stood outside. She walked up and reached for the doorknob.

"I'm sorry," said the cop on the left as he moved in front of the door. "No one is permitted in this room."

"Is that a medical request?" asked Mariah.

"Oakland Police Department."

"Mr. Stevens no longer works for any police department," stated Mariah.

"He is under investigation," answered the other cop. "We were instructed to allow no one into his room."

"But he may be dying!" Mariah pushed against the cop in front of the door. "I am his attorney."

"I'm sorry." The cop motioned with his head down the hallway. "Please have a seat. Or you can call my supervisor." He handed her a business card with the number of a police detective. Mariah left. She suddenly realized that she should not have left her car. Depending on how desperate these police were, they might be breaking into it while she argued with the cops in front of Stevens' room.

She was relieved to see her car intact. Looking around for any cars that might be watching her, she left the parking lot and headed north towards Telegraph and Dwight Way. She rang Peter's cell.

"Hey," Peter answered. He could hear Mariah's rather rapid breathing. "What's wrong?"

"Stevens is in the hospital. His room is guarded. The cops guarding it told me he is under investigation." She was breathing more evenly now. "I'm not going to your place in case I'm being followed. How about we meet up in Richmond? At El Tapatio?"

"All right. See ya'." Peter hung up. He looked around his apartment to make sure there was no weed anywhere and locked the door. This was certainly taking a turn toward the weird, he thought.

Twenty minutes later they were in a booth in the back of the restaurant. The owner was a client of Mariah's and promised them everything on the house. He would not let anybody near them. They each sipped on a Tecate. Peter's without lemon and Mariah's with. After she finished the bottle, two more were set on the table. She leaned back and related her experience of the afternoon. The ambulance in the hospice lot. The receptionist. The missing documents and the cops at the door. Peter thought about what might be occurring behind the scenes while he listened to Mariah. Why were the cops suddenly interested in Stevens? Two combinacion especiales arrived at their table and they began eating. The waiter brought two more Tecates. After Mariah finished her burrito and frijoles, she looked over at Peter.

"I need to call Jasmin." she wiped her mouth. "The only way to uncover this is via the press. Stevens is probably already fuckin' dead. You know the cops will never tell us why they took him and what happened to those papers. If we can get Jasmin's station interested, perhaps they'll shine just enough light on those fuckers." She took out her cell and speed-dialed Jasmin. Peter finished up his plate. He hadn't realized how hungry he was. Mariah asked for two more Tecates while she waited for Jasmin to answer.

"Hey, Jasmin. This is Mariah." Peter deduced that she had gotten Jasmin's voicemail. "Call me as soon as you get this message. Thanks."

Peter squeezed some lemon into Mariah's beer and handed her the bottle. She took the bottle and squeezed his hand. He smiled.

"So, what's your theory?" he asked.

"My theory?" responded Mariah. "These cops are hiding something. Those documents that Stevens had copies of are obviously part of the key to whatever they're hiding."

"Do you think he really needs to be in a hospital or is he just there because it's easier for the cops to secure the place?" Peter took Mariah's plate and began eating the remaining enchiladas. He really was hungry.

"I don't know," answered Mariah. "If he isn't that sick, I wonder why he didn't answer any of my calls the past few days."

"Yeah. It's not like he's gonna' be intimidated by some cops," said Peter. "He's probably meaner than anyone who wears the uniform these days."

"But why go after him now?" Mariah was trying to apply her attorney's mind to the facts she knew. She thought of Paul Drake. Perry Mason's investigator had always been her favorite character on that show. Reruns played constantly on one of the cable channels. Her cell rang.

It was Jasmin. "Hey," said Mariah. "Something big has come up. Stevens is in the hospital under police guard."

"Why?" asked Jasmin.

"That's where you come in," answered Mariah. "Can you and Nguyen get over to the East Bay tonight?"

"We'll be there in an hour."

"Cool. Meet us at Telegraph and Dwight." Mariah hung up.

Mariah ordered some dessert and Peter had another beer. He called Esperanza to let her know what was up. "Keep the doors locked and don't let anyone in. We'll call when we get outside the building."

Peter left a tip and they left the restaurant.

Jasmin and Nguyen were on their way back to San Francisco. The cops guarding Stevens were as unresponsive as she expected. Her calls to their supervisor and the detective on the business card Mariah was handed were almost as fruitless. She did have information that Stevens was considered to be in possession of stolen police property. However, the nature of that property was not made known to Jasmin. She assumed that it was the documents Mariah had made copies of, but the police refused to say anything. Hospital personnel had told her that Mr. Stevens was in poor shape and might not make it through the night. His cancer had advanced surprisingly quick given his earlier diagnosis, but cancer did that sometimes. Her plan was to go home, edit the footage and do some more background. Hopefully, a story would come forward. If everything worked out, she could get something on the next day's six o'clock news.

Peter and Mariah were on their way to Mariah's apartment. When they arrived in the parking garage, Peter saw two unmarked police vehicles. He called Esperanza on his cell. She answered. Everything was okay in the building. Peter told her that he and Mariah were being watched.

"If we're not up in five minutes, call Jasmin," instructed Peter. "Do you have her number?"

"Yeah."

"Okay. Hopefully we'll see you in a couple minutes." Peter hung up. He and Mariah exited the car and headed toward the stairs. A man stepped from one of the unmarked vehicles. He walked towards the couple. Peter thought about ignoring him, but decided to stop. After all, Mariah was a lawyer.

"Excuse me, Ms. Callahan," said the plainclothesman. He produced his identification.

Mariah looked over the ID. "Yes, officer?"

"Mr. Stevens died thirty minutes ago. He asked me to let you know when that happened."

"Thanks." Mariah turned to go up the stairs.

"One more thing, Ms. Callahan." Mariah stopped and turned around.

"Yes?"

I believe you have something that you are not legally permitted to have." he moved a step forward. "It is the property of the OPD."

"Talk to me in court." Mariah turned sharply and headed toward the stairs. Peter followed. When they were safely inside Mariah's apartment she called Jasmin and told her about Stevens' death.

The next night. Channel Four 6 O'Clock News. One of the talking heads introduced the story about

Stevens. Then Jasmin appeared onscreen.

"Not too long ago, this station featured an interview with Esperanza Cruz as part of the Saturday Newsmagazine. Miss Cruz's interview was included in a segment regarding a man who died during last summer's disturbances at Santa Rita County Jail in Alameda County. Her father was the deceased. He was in Santa Rita awaiting trial on a twenty-seven year old murder charge." A clip from the interview played silently behind Jasmin as she spoke. "After that segment played, Mariah Callahan, Mr. Johnson's attorney, and others began a campaign looking into the circumstances surrounding the death of Mr. Johnson and the other men who died that night in Santa Rita. The investigation has been met with silence from prison authorities although Ms. Callahan and the other attorneys were able to obtain video from the prison's security cameras from that night."

"As regards the case for which Mr. Johnson was facing trial, the authorities seem to have let it die. Callahan, Ms. Cruz and other friends of the deceased have been doing some investigation of their own, but have found nothing conclusive. The source of one lead--a former undercover officer for what is now known as the California Bureau of Investigation--was working with Ms. Callahan and had in fact provided some revealing information regarding the man who may have been the actual murderer in that case so long ago. This source, named Richard Stevens, told Ms. Callahan in a conversation that was recorded that he believed the real killer was a man who worked for numerous police agencies as an informant. Stevens told Callahan, 'I know he killed him.'"

"Mr. Stevens died last night. Police were guarding his room at Alta Bates Hospital when the death occurred. Callahan had tried to meet with Stevens yesterday and was denied entrance, despite the fact the she was working as his attorney. Police have warned her away from following up on this case. It is believed that Stevens had provided Callahan with evidence regarding the man he believed to be the real suspect in the case that Johnson was facing trial for. This evidence had apparently been removed from police files . How Mr. Stevens came by the evidence is not known at this time."

Peter, Esperanza and Mariah watched the program at Peter's place. A cat Peter had named Porgy lay on Esperanza's lap. The three of them shared a bottle of wine. After the program they watched a DVD of an old favorite of Peter's called *Watermelon Man*.

Three Days Later

Mariah returned to her office Monday morning around 9. The building caretaker told her that her office door had been left unlocked over the weekend. Mariah told him she was certain she had locked up when she left last week. He suggested that perhaps the janitorial crew had forgotten to lock it.

"I don't know, Tyler," she answered. "That's never happened before."

"I'll check on it for you," he told her. "They do have a couple new folks working on the weekend crew."

"Thanks, Tyler." she got in the elevator.

"Call me if anything is missing."

"I will." The elevator door closed and Mariah headed up to her floor.

She did not see anything out of place when she opened the door. After placing her bag and laptop on the desk in her office, she looked around the front room carefully. All of the papers on the desk seemed to be where she left them. The desk drawers were locked as always. She went into her office. At first glance, nothing seemed out of place. She sat down at her desk and began slowly opening the drawers. The papers seemed a bit more orderly than they usually were, but not extraordinarily so. Mariah may have straightened them out herself while talking on the phone or engaged in another activity. She took her laptop out of its case and turned it on. After going through its boo-tup procedure she tried to connect to the wireless. Nothing. She went into the front office and took a look at the router connected to the main workstation there. The router appeared to be working. All the lights that were supposed to be on were lit. She unplugged the power and plugged it back in. Then she went back into her office and tried to connect. No luck. She went back into the front office and picked up the router. The case looked like it had been opened. She decided to try and open her email on the main workstation that her assistant used. No problem. She composed a quick message to Peter just to see if email could be sent. The message went out. Peter responded within a minute. Nothing wrong there. Maybe the cleaning crew had just been careless. Since she had no court appointments, she might as well take the router to Best Buy or somewhere and buy a new one. She called Tyler. On her way out of the building, she told Tyler what she had found. He told her he would talk to the cleaning crew manager.

Mariah didn't really think she needed to be paranoid.

At least not any more than she was normally. However, the fact that her office door was found unlocked and her router stopped working raised her suspicions. Especially in light of the whole situation around Mr. Stevens' final day. She wondered if she should back up her laptop files or maybe go ahead and buy a new one to use. That way, she could put the one she had with her in a safe place until she had some definite answers on this whole thing around Porgy. It seemed that her investigation into his cause of death was not the real concern of the police. However her investigation of the old murder charges and the possibility that Porgy was falsely charged to protect one of their informers seemed to have put something in motion.

She exited I-80 near Emeryville and began to look for Mandela Parkway. She could see the big box stores ahead of her. She had no sooner parked her car in the lot near Best Buy when a couple of young black men in suits appeared in front of her.

"Hey sister," said the one to her left. He was about six feet tall and perhaps 180 pounds. The other man was a few inches shorter and a bit stouter.

Mariah looked at both of them. "Yes?"

The taller man produced a badge. "California Bureau of Investigation. Barry Jackson. This is my partner, Al Brooks."

Mariah nodded to the two men. "How can I help you?"

"We need to talk with you about the matter of Richard Stevens," said Barry. "We understand he was in contact with you in the months before he died."

Mariah said nothing. She took her laptop and the router out of the car and closed the door. She locked the doors with her automatic lock and headed towards the store. The men followed her.

"We have permission to take you in," warned Jackson.

"I doubt that," said Mariah. She continued walking towards the store's entrance. She was walking fast. She was about fifty feet away.

"Brooks sped up his gait. He was walking next to Mariah. "Look,' he said. "we know you have some copies of documents regarding a former informant for several California police agencies. Those documents have been sealed and are in your possession illegally. You can choose to hand them over now or you can face an indictment for several felonies. Mr. Stevens received those papers through illegal means. When he died he was under arrest, as was the person who gave the documents to him."

Mariah continued walking. "Look,' she said. "I would not give you those documents even if I had them. It's obvious they contain some highly sensitive information that the state does not want revealed. Perhaps they even contain some information that reveals criminal behavior on the part of the police. No matter what, however, I am not going to hand them back to you or anyone else without a fight."

Brooks grabbed her arm. Mariah yanked away from him and yelled loudly. "Leave me alone!" Her voice caused several people in the parking lot and near the store entrance to look around. Brooks and Jackson dropped back. Mariah entered the store. While she shopped for another laptop and router, she considered what had just occurred. It was quite obvious that she needed to keep copies of the documents somewhere else besides her home or office. Too bad the documents did not clear Porgy. They only made it clear that Ra's criminality did not effect his status as an informant. Furthermore, his status as an informant allowed him to get away with criminal activities consistently. She wondered how the documents had been traced to her possession.

Esperanza was at Mariah's. She had the day off and was taking it easy. Cleaning up the apartment and listening to music. The buzzer sounded. She went over and pressed the intercom.

"Hello?" There was no answer. She pressed it again. Still no answer. She went back to cleaning. The buzzer sounded again. She pushed the intercom. Still no answer. She wished there was a window that she could look out of and see who it was. She decided to ignore it and went back to cleaning. Perhaps five minutes later there was a knock on the apartment door. Esperanza walked to the door and asked who it was.

"Oakland Police Department." Esperanza opened the door slightly. She saw a woman in uniform and her hand showing her badge.

"Yes?" asked Esperanza.

"Is Mariah Callahan home?" asked the cop.

Esperanza told her no and began to close the door. The cop's foot was in the way. "Who are you?" she demanded.

Esperanza felt like telling her to go to hell. Instead she gave the cop her name.

"Do you live here?" asked the cop.

"I am staying here right now," answered Esperanza. She wished the cop would move her foot. Then she could close the door and call Mariah.

"Are you a US citizen?" asked the cop.

"My father is." The phone was ringing. Esperanza wanted to answer it but feared that the cop would enter the apartment if Esperanza left the door.

"Tell Ms. Callahan to call me," said the cop. "Here is my card." She handed Esperanza a business card and left. Esperanza locked the door. Fuckin' cops.

Late That Night

Peter, Mariah and Esperanza were in San Francisco. For security's sake, they had rented a couple rooms at a motel near the ocean. It was a mile or two from the motel Peter had stayed at back in 1980 when moonshadow turned herself in. After Mariah and Esperanza went over the day's experiences with the police, the three of them decided it would be best to get out of the East Bay for a day or two. The plan was for the three of them to spend a couple nights at the motel and for Peter to check in on Mariah's apartment and office during the day. They had spent the evening at the motel watching baseball and drinking beer. While the game was on they discussed the day's events. Mariah had brought all of the DVDs and documents related to Porgy with her.

Noon the Following Day

Peter was at Mariah's apartment. Everything seemed to be in order. He grabbed a couple books she had asked for and a CD for Esperanza and left. Next stop was Mariah's office. He parked the car he was driving and locked it up. Tyler was outside the building enjoying the sunshine. Peter said hello.

"Mariah's been getting a lot of police visitors," he told Peter. "Her assistant is there today and she must be sending them away as quick as they come in 'cause they sure ain't stayin' long." Peter smiled and thanked him for the information. He went upstairs. The front door was unlocked so he walked in. Mariah's assistant Susan looked up.

"Hey Peter."

"Hey. How you doing, Susan?"

"Okay," she answered. "How's Mariah?"

"She's all right. Any interesting calls or visitors?" Peter picked up the mail from the desk. Mariah would want to look at that.

"I just got off the phone with Mariah and told her

that different cops keep on showing up here looking for her. I just keep sending them away."

"Good."

"What are they so interested in Mariah for all of a sudden?" asked Susan.

"It has to do with that pro bono case she's so into," answered Peter.

"That Porgy Johnson one?"

"Yeah. Seems like there's a lot of stuff the cops don't want anybody to know."

"They sure have been coming around." She handed Peter a list of numbers and names. "Here's the cops that came around and here are some phone calls she should return. Tell her and Esperanza hi."

"I will." Peter left.

Next stop was his apartment. He got in the car and headed towards Berkeley. On the way, he saw Rain walking. He slowed down.

"You going to Telegraph?" he asked.

"Yeah. Hey Peter!" Rain opened the passenger door and climbed in.

"I'm going to my place for a couple minutes," said Peter. "I can let you off."

"How you been?"

"Okay." Peter slowed the car. There was some kind of accident up ahead.

"Did you ever see Nathaniel?" asked Rain.

"Yeah. He's doing okay. He helped me out with that thing too."

"You getting anywhere with it?"

"Not really," answered Peter. "Although we did get a ton of video from the riot. It seems to show Porgy dying after a bunch of tear gas was pumped into the cage he was shackled."

"Fuckin' pigs." The traffic was moving again. At the corner of Dwight and Telegraph, Rain looked over to Peter. "See ya' Peter." She kissed him and got out. Peter went up to Haste Street and looked for a place to park. He decided he would walk from there to his place. After parking he walked to Milvia and took a left. Then a right on Dwight Way. As he approached his apartment building he noticed a pair of men sitting on the steps. They didn't look like tenants. Both appeared to be in their late fifties. He walked past them.

"Excuse me, sir," said one of the men. "Can we talk?" Peter looked. He shrugged.

"Sure. I guess." He remained standing.

"Do you know Mariah Callahan?" asked the guy closest to Peter. Peter nodded.

"We need something she has." Only one guy was talking. The other one sat there looking around a bit nervous.

"I'm just a friend," said Peter.

"I don't think so," said the talker. "We know that you came out here because she asked you to help her on the Porgy Johnson murder trial. We also know that you were a friend of Johnson. We're not sure what role you may have played in his escape from justice back in

1980, but we could probably make something up to keep you in jail long enough to make you wish you had cooperated."

"Who the fuck are you?" asked Peter. He tried to walk past them. The quiet one stood up and pushed him back.

"Let's just say we're interested in seeing the Johnson case put back to rest," said the talker. "Permanently."

Peter didn't say anything. The noise of the breaking glass at the recycling center crashed in the background. "Are you cops?"

"You could say that," answered the talker. "You could say we're independent contractors."

That didn't sound good. It reminded Peter of the guys that killed Iraqis and Afghans at will. He knew that being independent meant these guys could do whatever they wanted to and were answerable to no one. He looked away.

"Can we go inside?" asked the talker. "Your door is already open."

"Motherfuckers," said Peter. He walked ahead. The two men followed him. Once inside, they sat on the couch. Peter grabbed a chair and sat. "What do you want from me?"

"We want those papers from your girlfriend," said the talker. "We don't care how you get them. Tell her that we'll put you away if she doesn't give them to us or just steal them. We don't give a shit."

"What I don't understand," began Peter. "is why

you want the papers. They're just copies and she could have already scanned them and stored them somewhere on the web or in her flash drive."

"We want her to know that if she doesn't give us every copy and destroy the non-paper ones we will destroy her law practice. Furthermore, we will see that Esperanza Cruz is deported after spending several months in one of the INS detention centers. Those aren't pretty places. Especially for such a pretty girl. As for you, we can fix up something to lock you away until you're seventy."

"Yeah, right," said Peter. "Where do you think you have this power?"

The quiet one looked at Peter. "PATRIOT Act, for starters."

"Think about it," said the talker. "Tell your girlfriend." The men turned and left. On the way out, the quiet one threw a bag of marijuana at Peter. "Oh yeah," he laughed. "This is yours."

Peter looked around the apartment. Nothing appeared to have been disturbed. The weed had been in one of the kitchen cupboards. Those assholes were just trying to intimidate him. To be honest, they had. This whole thing must be bigger than what he or Mariah thought. He needed to get back to San Francisco, but he didn't want to be followed. Of course, they could find out where they were by tracing the cell phone calls from the motel. Time to buy some throwaways.

Peter was back at the motel. The ride by bus had taken a couple hours. He stopped at a drug store and bought three throwaways and some phone cards for himself, Mariah and Esperanza. Mariah planned on taking their regular cells to her office and leaving them there for the time being. He told the women what had happened and what had been said. Mariah got on her throwaway and talked to an older man who was a friend and mentor. He was an experienced civil liberties attorney in San Rafael by the name of Bert Schutzholm. Had been friends with her parents. She wanted to know what she was up against. The conversation went on for thirty minutes. Mariah did not seem relieved when she hung up.

"Well," she began. "We better watch our asses. Whoever is after us really wants to intimidate us into dropping the idea to clear Porgy's name. There's obviously something bigger than just Porgy and a false murder charge here. Bert said it sounded like we may have touched on a previously unknown element of COINTELPRO. Those guys who confronted you, Peter, were probably some kind of feds or contractors--most likely the latter."

"Like in Iraq?" asked Esperanza.

"Yeah," said Mariah.

"That means they weren't joking when they said they could pretty much do what they wanted to get us to stop," thought Peter aloud.

"Bert also said that we should move around every

couple days and, if we wanted, we could stay at his place in Marin," said Mariah. "It's totally secure according to him."

"What about the case?" asked Peter. He wasn't ready to give up on Porgy just yet.

"He said to hang in there," answered Mariah. "Judging from the reaction of the cops, chances are we are pretty close to the final piece. Of course, what that piece is we have no idea. If Stevens had lived, he might have been able to guide us to some information that clearly pointed the finger at Ra. The chances of that happening now are pretty much nil. Unless..."

"Unless, what?" asked Esperanza.

"Unless we can find somebody else in law enforcement who was involved in covering up for Ra," answered Mariah. "However, people like Ra usually didn't have more than one handler. Less chance of anybody's cover being blown."

"Plausible deniability, too," interjected Peter.

"Yeah."

"Let's get some food," suggested Peter. The women agreed. They left the motel for an Italian place a couple miles away. Nobody seemed to be following them. The documents and DVDs were in Mariah's bag.

January 28, 2008

Mariah was scheduled to defend in court three days this week. She showed up for her first arraignment at 9 AM on Monday. She was met by the bailiff who told her that she had been removed from her first two cases. They were public defender cases. One was a drug sales charge and the other was a DUI. She asked the bailiff why, but he told her he had no idea. Oh well, things like that happened. Her next case was slated for the afternoon. She had met with the defendant three times. It was a burglary charge that involved a couple upper middle class twenty year-olds who were accused of burglarizing homes in their Oakland Hills neighborhood. The parents had paid her five thousand up front. She waited in the hall for the young man to arrive. When he did, his parents walked up to where she was waiting.

"Ms. Callahan," the father began. "I want to thank you for your services, but we have found another attorney."

"What?" asked Mariah. "Why? I believe I can get

your son a reasonable diversion offer."

"It's not you or your work, Ms. Callahan." He walked away. The mother did not look at Mariah. Their son whispered to his mom. She left. He turned to Mariah.

"It's weird, Ms. Callahan," he began. "My parents were talking about how good you were last Monday. Then dad comes home from work on Thursday and tells me and Mom that he got another attorney for me. I asked him why and he said that some men who visited his office suggested my chances might not be too good if they kept you."

"Some men?" asked Mariah. "Do you know who they were?"

"Dad didn't say nothing else about it," said the young man. "I figured it was one of those times when you just let it drop."

"Thanks," said Mariah. "Good luck on your trial." She called her office. Susan answered. "Hi Susan. Have I received any calls?"

"Hi Mariah." Susan looked at her Blackberry. "It's weird, but three people have called just this morning to say they are switching to different lawyers. None of them gave me a reason, but Isabella Goldberg said that she had been warned not to use your services. When I asked her who warned her, she just said she got a phone call."

"Thanks, Susan. I'll see you in about an hour."

So, thought Mariah, this is what they do. They're

fucking with me. Fortunately for me it's just money. For Esperanza or Peter it's their lives. Motherfuckers. Sure didn't take them long. She left the courthouse. Maybe she would be back tomorrow if she had any clients left by then.

Mariah and Esperanza were at Bert's in Marin. Peter was meeting Arlo and Bonita for lunch. It was a Mexican place in Alameda. He ordered a bucket of Coronitas while he waited. The waiter brought the beers and some chips and salsa. Peter opened a beer. Ten minutes later, the two walked in. Arlo sat down and grabbed a beer from the bucket. Bonita ordered a margarita.

"So, man." Arlo looked around the restaurant. "Have the cops been fuckin' with you anymore?" Peter had told Arlo the entire saga about the cops, contractors, Stevens, the documents and his death.

"Nah," said Peter. "But I know it's just a matter of time. I've been keeping clean as a whistle. Been taking buses a lot and just laying low. I'm more concerned about Mariah and Esperanza though. They gotta' go to work which means they're much more visible."

"You guys can stay at our place if you want," offered Bonita.

"Thanks." Peter didn't want to bring any heat down on his friends, especially since he didn't know exactly who he was dealing with.

"How do you think they found out about the

documents?" asked Arlo.

"I'm guessing they intimidated the person who gave them to Stevens.' said Peter. "Either that, or whoever that was was trying to set Stevens up and told the investigators right off."

"Can't trust a cop," said Arlo.

"Not very often," agreed Peter. They ordered some lunch combo plates and continued drinking.

"Oh yeah." Arlo reached into his back pocket and pulled out some money. He handed it to Peter. "This is from Michael. He said good luck. If you need a place to stash your shit or whatever, he said you could use one of his storage facilities. I could take it there for you."

"I'm gonna' keep my place," said Peter. "If this blows over, I'll be fine."

"And if it doesn't?" asked Bonita.

"I guess I'll be leaving." answered Peter. "I would like to clear Porgy's name, though. And get some kind of closure on his death."

"How's that going?" asked Arlo.

"Well, we have the footage that shows Porgy collapsing and dying after the cage he was in was pumped full of tear gas. The attorneys representing the other fatalities' families are trying to figure out how to proceed. They know that Mariah's been tangled up in this constantly growing mess. Hopefully, we'll at least get some kind of settlement and admission of negligence or wrongdoing before summer."

"What do you mean--constantly growing mess?"

asked Bonita.

Peter ran down the death of Stevens, the intimidation by police agents and others, the loss of clients by Mariah, and the traveling road show that his, Mariah and Esperanza's life had become.

"Where are the women right now?" asked Bonita. She finished her margarita and motioned to the waiter for another.

"At a friend of Mariah's up in Marin," answered Peter. "He's this guy in his seventies who's used to police harassment. His fuckin' place is like a medium security joint. Cameras, sensors, the whole deal. He used to be a lawyer for the Panthers, the Weather Underground, the Brotherhood of Eternal Love and the SLA."

"He knows his shit, then," guessed Arlo.

"He knows his shit," agreed Peter.

"What about you?" asked Bonita. "Aren't you worried?"

"Eh. Whatever," answered Peter. "I'd rather they took me down than those two. I could pretend like I had all the goods they were looking for and then maybe they'd let those two get back to their lives."

"You can stay at our place tonight," said Bonita. "Just let the girls know where you are."

"Thanks." Peter took out his throwaway. Arlo took it from him. "What are you doing?" asked Peter.

"I don't trust them motherfuckers over at the bar," answered Arlo. Peter looked over. The two contractors from the scene at his apartment sat there. The talker and the quiet one. Somehow Peter had missed their entry.

"Thanks, bro. Those guys are no good."

"Let's get our of here," said Arlo. "Go to the bathroom and climb out the window. I know the manager here. Me and Bonita eat here a lot, plus I take my clients here. I'll ask him to keep those fuckers at the bar. Our car is parked two streets over in a friend's driveway. We'll be there in about five minutes.'

"Cool. Thanks." Peter headed toward the restroom. Ten minutes later the three of them were on their way back to the Oakland Hills. Arlo looked in his rear view mirror.

"Geez, Peter," laughed Bonita. "It's like some freaking movie. Fucking undercover tailing us and everything."

"Like the old days, huh."

"Yeah," joked Arlo. "Remember when were going to that big Dead show in Jersey and we were driving around Snowdon looking to buy some acid? The cops pulled us over like they were SWAT and Mark jumped out of the car like he was some gangster. Then, when they didn't find anything the cops told us to get the hell out of town that night...."

"Which worked out just fine. "said Bonita. "Since we were driving up to the concert that night." Arlo pulled into their driveway. They waited ten minutes. No cars appeared. The three got out of the car and Peter called Mariah to let them know his whereabouts.

February 11, 2008--Two Weeks Later

Mariah had spent only three days in court over the past two weeks. Usually, she would have spent at least twice as many. Esperanza's boss had told her that INS had been by asking about her. She was given some time off. Peter's apartment had been ransacked. Of course, nothing was there worth taking but the message was clear. Peter felt he could ignore it if it weren't for Mariah and Esperanza. Although Peter had stayed at his place three or four nights, Mariah and Esperanza visited Mariah's apartment only during the day. She had instructed Tyler to record the name of anyone who visited her office. He did so faithfully. The log revealed very little. Postal carriers. Potential clients. Two incidences of unnamed men with government IDs. Tyler told Mariah that he had followed the men by going up the stairs to ensure they didn't try any funny business. Mariah wondered if they were planting surveillance devices. She refused to conduct any business in her office.

Early the Next Evening

Mariah was leaving a meeting in downtown Oakland with the attorneys for the other families whose men had died at Santa Rita. A decision had been reached to sue the county. They were going to ask the DA to file criminal charges against the individual guards shown in the video to be firing their weapons recklessly. Mariah's efforts in obtaining the video and cataloging the DVDs were roundly praised. She was asked how the attempts to clear Porgy's name were going. She said she preferred not to comment in a public venue. As she was leaving, she was approached by a middle-aged woman. Mariah had no idea who she was, but assumed she might be a relative of one of the killed inmates. She slowed down a bit to talk with her.

"Ms. Callahan." The woman hurried to catch up. "I have something."

Mariah looked around. Her recent experiences with strangers had made her a little wary. The door was not far.

"This is from my stepfather's brother, Dick Stevens." She handed Mariah a business size envelope.

Mariah jammed it in her bag. The woman walked away quickly. Mariah wished she had come to the meeting with someone else. She walked quickly outside and to her car. Once inside the automobile, she locked the doors and started the engine. She looked behind her. As arranged, Peter and Arlo were in Arlo's car. She pulled out and the men followed. They headed towards the Bay Bridge. When she pulled up to the toll booth, Peter and Arlo nodded at her from the adjacent booth. After reaching San Francisco, the two cars made their way toward North Beach. They parked a few blocks away and got out. Their destination was a bar a couple blocks down Broadway.

The three walked together. The night was cool for San Francisco but clear. As always, the sidewalks were full of people. Most of them were younger than Mariah and the men. She held her laptop close to her body like a schoolgirl holds her schoolbooks. The envelope she had been handed was tucked in her jacket's inside pocket. As they neared the bar, Arlo noticed two men coming up behind them rather quickly. He took Mariah's elbow and nudged her forward. She resisted at first before she realized why Arlo was pushing her. Just before they reached the door the man on the right grabbed Mariah's laptop. Peter took her inside the bar. Arlo gave chase until he saw them get into a car. He looked for a license number but the license was caked in mud. The car was a brown mid 1990s Toyota Camry with a missing left tail light. He headed back to the bar.

Mariah and Peter had a booth on the left side of the bar. The bar itself formed an oval without one end in the middle of the building. Arlo sat down. When the waitress came he ordered a shot of Maker's Mark. A Lightnin' Hopkins CD was playing on the sound system.

"Are you okay?" Arlo asked Mariah. She looked pretty relaxed considering she had just been attacked.

"Yeah. I'm fine," she replied. "You know, I let them have that laptop."

"What do you mean?"

"I gave it up, Arlo," she repeated. "Everything I needed from that hard drive I have stored somewhere else or I sent it to my email from that meeting. They can have that machine. It won't give whoever they're working for anything I don't have."

She looked around the bar. Esperanza was supposed to be here with a guy she was seeing. She hoped she was okay. Arlo called Bonita.

"Besides," continued Mariah. "I think I've got the real prize in my coat pocket here." She tapped her jacket. The two men looked at her questioningly. "Right when I was leaving that meeting in Oakland a woman gave me an envelope she said was from Stevens."

"But he's dead," Arlo said quietly

"She told me it came via her stepfather--Stevens's brother."

"Have you looked at it?" asked Peter.

"No freakin' way." Mariah looked around again. Still no Esperanza. "I'm waiting until I get back to Marin and inside Bert's house. By the way Peter, you coming back there with me tonight?"

Peter wanted to. It had been a couple weeks since they had been together. He didn't think it was a good idea even yet. However, unless she was going by taxi or Bert sent a car, he wasn't going to let her and Esperanza drive to San Rafael by themselves.

"Isn't Esperanza supposed to meet you here?" asked Peter.

Mariah nodded. "She should be here by now." Arlo looked toward the door. He wasn't certain, but he thought he saw Esperanza entering the bar. "Isn't that her?" Mariah looked to where he pointed. She breathed a sigh of relief. Esperanza was okay. Nobody was with her, though. She waved. Esperanza came over. Arlo moved over in the booth and Esperanza sat down.

"Where's your hombre, Ramon?" asked Mariah.

"La migra," answered Esperanza.

"What? They took him?" asked Mariah.

"Yeah," answered Esperanza. "Fuckin' ICE raid."

"Was he illegal?" asked Peter.

"Yo no lo creo," said Esperanza. "I don't think so,"

"Then why...?"

"I don't know," answered Esperanza. "He called me before they put everyone on the bus and took away their cells. He said it might have something to do with his political work in Oaxaca."

"Why? What was he doing there?" asked Peter.

"Remember that teacher's strike in 2006 that turned into a general strike and then the army came in and disappeared a bunch of people? He was one of the APPA organizers."

"Shit," said Mariah. "And they're sending him back to the cops down there?"

"Looks like they are," answered Esperanza. "You know, he went to the same school I went to except he's five years older than me."

"He doesn't look that old," noted Mariah. They had another drink. Peter insisted that Mariah call Bert and arrange for him to send a car. An hour or so after she called, Bert came into the bar and bought a round for the four of them and himself. Then the women left with Bert and his driver.

The women were in Marin at Bert's. The ride home had been uneventful. Mariah removed the envelope from her jacket. The envelope contained a few sheets of paper. Some were lined. Others looked like official forms. Mariah unfolded them The top one was handwritten.

Ms. Callahan, it began. *The documents here are originals. They were given to me a little over three years ago by the officer who succeeded me in "handling' Ronnie Freedman (Ra). According to this officer (now deceased) the document was supposed to be destroyed back when it was written in 1986. The officer told me he assumed that he would be asked to turn over the document and that it would be destroyed by higher-ups in the agency. So, he made Freedman write out two statements and sign them both. This is the one that the officer kept. According to the officer, the statements were identical. My brother was given these for safekeeping before I went into the hospice. I instructed him to get them to you if I died.*

Mariah handed the first page to Bert. The next page was a blank piece of lined writing paper. She set that one on the table. The next was a cover sheet with the following information.

Statement from "Ra" Ronnie Freedman. July 16, 1986
Written in the presence of Detective Joshua Mandel CBI, CHP
Signed: Det. J. Mandel

The next page was a standard confession sheet written in Ra's hand. It read:

> *Sometime during the month of March 1980 I drove Rosa McNamara to a house in Marin County near San Rafael. The purpose of the ride was to help McNamara buy a large amount of LSD. At the time I was working undercover infiltrating the radical group NPLF in Berkeley. I did not know that McNamara was also undercover for a different agency. After dropping her off, I went to San Rafael and had a few drinks at a bar in the downtown. Around midnight I drove back to the house and picked McNa-*

mara up at the end of the long driveway. This was where I left her off before. She was thirsty so I gave her some juice I was drinking. I had put a red and maybe something else in it just to get myself a buzz. She drank the whole bottle. On the way home I left the highway and stopped in a wooded area. I then tried to have sex with McNamara. She refused and told me she had a boyfriend. I kept on trying because I didn't believe her. Besides, she and I had "played" around a little before. She hit me hard with a book that was in the car. I lost my temper and hit her a few times until she stopped moving. She was still breathing and even kissed me when I fucked her. When I was done I tried to wake her up but she seemed to be unconscious. I got scared and got back on the freeway. When we got past San Quentin I pulled over and threw her out of the car because I was afraid she was dead. I never told anyone what happened until now.
Signed,
Ronnie Freedman
July 16, 1986
Joshua Mandel
July 16, 1986

The last sheet of paper was a note from Mandel.

Richard, this is the statement from "Ra" Freedman. When I submitted the confession to the agency, I was told that the case was closed and that the murderer was a fugitive believed to be in Mexico. Freedman

"So, " said Mariah. "This is it. The smoking gun. Now to get someone in the system to listen."

"If that doesn't happen? asked Bert.

"What do you mean?"

"If you can't find someone in the system?"

"To consider our case?"

"Yes.' said Bert.

"I don't know," answered Mariah. "The press?"

"They won't touch this," answered Bert. "It's like the Black Panthers in the Sixties. The mainstream media refused to write about them except in the context of their criminality. Naturally, this meant they ignored the criminality of the police."

Esperanza stood up and stretched. "I'm going to bed. I've gotta' get up in the morning and get to the Mission."

"I'll give you a ride in," Bert told her.

"Thanks."

February 13, 2008

Esperanza waited outside a church on Mission. Bert had dropped her off ten minutes earlier. She insisted he leave, so he did. It was early morning and she was supposed to meet some friends. Several vans were parked along the street and there were very few pedestrians. Given that the churches and the Mission itself were usually quite alive most of the time, she thought the calm unusual. She heard her friends up the street. Most of them were on their way to work but were heading to breakfast first. No sooner had they reached where Esperanza stood when the rear doors of several of the vans opened and men dressed entirely in black and carrying guns jumped out. "La Migra! La Migra!" Esperanza's friends scattered, darting into doorways, alleys and the open doors of stores and churches. The police ran in groups of two chasing down and trapping individuals. Once they were caught, La Migra cops bound their wrists with plastic handcuffs and pushed them towards a bus that had suddenly appeared. Esperanza called Mariah on her phone. "ICE raid...!" was all she said before an ICE agent grabbed her from behind. She tried to put the phone in her pocket, but was unsuccessful. After binding her wrists, the agent reached down and picked up the phone. He placed it in his vest pocket and led her to the waiting bus. Thirty minutes later, the bus full of arrestees was on its way to the Bryant Street jail.

Once the bus arrived, the arrestees were processed and put six into a cell. Esperanza was placed with five other women and teenage girls from the raid. One woman was crying and pleading with the matron to let her contact her children's babysitter. The matron promised she would see what she could do. Esperanza noted that she actually seemed sympathetic. She wondered what would happen next. Would they be deported or shipped to a more long-term detention facility? She thought about Ramon. She sat back on the steel bed and listened to the sounds of the jail. The woman who was pleading earlier was now sobbing softly. Esperanza hoped that Mariah would understand her abbreviated phone message.

Mariah finished a conference call with the other attorneys involved in the wrongful deaths at Santa Rita. The preliminary discussions with the DA's office were not hopeful. In short, he was determined not to bring criminal charges of any kind against the officers in the prison or their superiors. Bert had intimated that this would be the case. Mariah and the other attorneys had decided to go above the county level and see if they could convince someone in the State Attorney General's office to look at the request to indict. If they were turned down there, a civil suit was definite. Her throwaway had buzzed while she was in the conference call. She checked her messages. The number was Esperanza's current throwaway. Mariah pressed in the code and heard Esperanza's brief, furtive shout--"La Migra!" She also heard the sound of people running, traffic, and shouting. She tried calling Esperanza back. No answer. Her next call was to the San Francisco Police Department.

After the phone was picked up, she was put on hold. She pushed a couple of buttons as directed and was soon talking to an officer, "Yes, San Francisco Police Department. How can I help you?"

Mariah phrased her question as neutrally as possible. Even though the department was forbidden by city law to assist the immigration authorities, one could never be certain about any particular cop's views on the situation. "Was there a raid by immigration agents in the Mission District this morning?"

"Let me check," answered the officer. "I'll be right back." Mariah heard the clicking of a keyboard. She waited. A minute or so later, the voice answered. "Yes, ma'am. At approximately 8:30 AM, thirty individuals were apprehended by INS agents."

"Do you know where they were taken?" asked Mariah.

"Bryant Street, ma'am."

"Thank you, officer." Mariah hung up. She called Bert. He promised to head into the city immediately. Mariah left her office and got into her car. She headed towards the Bay Bridge. When she got to Bryant Street, she found a place to park and headed inside the jail building. Bert was already there. He was talking with another attorney and an INS official. Mariah entered their circle.

"Sirs," the INS official was saying to Bert and the other attorney. "Your clients will remain in our custody until we establish their identities and their right to be in the United States. If we can establish that within twenty-four hours they will be released. Otherwise, they will be sent to an INS facility for further detention until their situation is determined."

"I demand that my client and any detainees with children in their care be released now," said Bert, his voice raised.

"I'm sorry." the INS official shook his head. "That will not be done until we establish their legal right to reside in this country."

Mariah was steaming. She wanted to see Esperanza. "Can we at least see her?"

"Who are you, ma'am?" asked the INS official.

"Attorney Mariah Callahan," answered Mariah. "Who are you?"

"Ralph Hunter, INS attorney." He extended his hand. Mariah shook it. "Does Ms. Cruz have two attorneys, then?" He nodded at Bert. "Mr. Schutzholm is also representing her."

"She's a fortunate individual," said Bert. "Much more than most of the people your agents remove so rudely from their lives."

"Just doing my assigned job, sir." Bert wanted to say something obvious like so was Adolf Eichmann, but he knew it would not help their cause. He refrained.

"And we are doing ours," responded Bert. "We will be here until Ms. Cruz's situation --and the situation of the other detainees--is resolved."

He and Mariah sat on some chairs nearby. The other defense attorney asked Bert to keep him abreast of the situation, gave Bert his client's name and said he had to be back in court. He left the hallway.

Peter's throwaway was ringing. He removed it from his pocket. It was Mariah.

"Hey, how you doing?" he asked.

"Not good," answered Mariah. "INS got Esperanza."

"Shit! You serious?" This was one of Peter's fears. "Where you at?"

"Bryant Street jail," answered Mariah. "You know it?"

"Oh yeah." Peter had spent a couple nights there back in 1977. Bullshit pot bust. "Should I come over there?"

"Probably not," answered Mariah. "Bert's here and he's working both ends of the situation. It would be nice to see you though."

"I agree. My dreams have been getting out of hand."

"Mine too." Mariah looked up. Bert was talking to

some official looking guy. "I'll call you once I know something. Where are you at?"

"Your place," answered Peter. "Just checking in with Tyler and all."

"See you sweetie." Mariah ended the call. Bert was arguing with the official. Mariah walked over to the two men.

"That's nonsense and you know it." Bert's voice had notched up a few decibels. The official--who Mariah now saw was from the INS--backed up a couple steps.

"I'm sorry, Mr. Schutzholm." The INS official looked at Mariah. "But your client stays here. I will let you know if she is to be shipped to Tacoma." Tacoma was the site of the Northwest Regional ICE Detention Facility. Bert turned and walked away. He was pissed. Mariah followed him. The two left the hallway.

"Let's go get some lunch," suggested Bert. Mariah followed him out of the building.

They were in a restaurant. Bert ordered a beer. Mariah ordered iced tea. Bert waited until his beer came, took a long drink and then began.

"The INS is saying that Esperanza is in the country illegally. Because the surname on her green card is Cruz and that name has been proven to be a false name assumed by her father who was a fugitive and in Mexico illegally the green card is invalid. Consequently, she will be deported."

"So," wondered Mariah. "If we follow that logic, then she doesn't exist in Mexico either. Correct?"

"I guess so," answered Bert. "Does that make her a stateless person? If it does, what could that mean?"

"Some anarchists would be envious," joked Mariah.

"The idea, while appealing, " began Bert. "Is actually nightmarish. Without citizenship, one is protected by nothing. One of the first things the Nazis did to the Jews was to take away their citizenship. This meant that they had no right to own property in Germany and ultimately no right to live there. The Israelis have done something similar to the Palestinians, the Europeans did it to the indigenous peoples here, and, on a smaller scale, that is the reasoning behind the various designations of our current government regarding its captives in their war on terror. In essence, without legal citizenship somewhere, one is subject to the whims of whatever authority they end up under. Esperanza's situation isn't good. If they send her back to Mexico, she may be able to get her citizenship back there via her mother's permanent residence there. If she stays here, I don't know how she can do so legally."

February 14, 2008

Peter was in a Berkeley cop car. It had been a while, but not long enough. The cops in the front seat had accosted him on his way to Telegraph from his apartment. Back in the 1970s, the Berkeley cops would take selected individuals up to Tilden Park and beat them. Peter hoped that wasn't the intention of these two despite the fact that they were on Euclid Avenue now and heading in that direction.

"I bet you're wondering where we're heading," said the driver, a big guy probably in his thirties.

 Peter said nothing. He figured he would let the cops do the talking.

"We know you must have had some friends back in the old days who took rides with our predecessors." This from the cop on the passenger side. A smaller fellow who looked part Chinese. Peter remained silent.

"Yeah," continued the guy riding shotgun. "We did some checking up on you. You were a reasonably popular guy in the BPD back then. Drug busts, political BS, and a big mouth." The car was in the hills now.

Soon they would be past the houses and in Tilden Park. Peter had watched many a sunset from different vantage points in that park, often under the influence of various psychoactive drugs.

The cruiser stopped. The driver turned around. "Get out," he said. "Now." Peter waited for the door to open. He stood up and stretched. The smaller cop had his hand on his nightstick. Peter looked around for a place to run. The cop went through his pockets and took Peter's throwaway.

"Don't worry," said the driver. "We aren't here to hurt you." He pushed on Peter's shoulders. "We are just helping out our friends in the OPD and other agencies. Word is that you and your lawyer friends are digging up some cases that are dead. Closed. Our message is, leave them that way." The cops got back in their cruiser and left. As they pulled away, the cop driving yelled out the window. "They told me to tell you that they'll find those papers you have, too."

Peter was a long way from home. He began to walk. If he wasn't so pissed off, he might find the situation humorous.

February 18, 2008

Barack Obama was winning big this primary season. Did it mean anything that a black man might be president? Peter and Mariah weren't so sure. They discussed it often. The only thing certain was the symbolism of a black man in the White House. Mariah opened her laptop to check her email. A message from one of the lawyers involved in the Santa Rita suit was first in her inbox. She opened it.

Mariah, it read, we have presented our case to the District Attorney's office asking for criminal charges to be brought against the deputies involved in the deaths of our clients. In addition, we have asked for negligence charges to be brought against their supervisors. The DA's answer was a very firm and definite no. Not only does he have no intention of filing charges, our request for a grand jury was also rejected. This seems to leave us two other possible courses. The first is to go to the State Attorney General and ask them to pursue charges. The second is to file a wrongful death suit against the county and the individual officers involved. After a brief discussion, Hal and I think the best route would be to approach the state, but also file the lawsuit. Perhaps we can reach a settlement outside of court that includes an admission of wrongdoing. The potentiality of the state filing charges may help the county authorities choose a settlement.

Mariah wrote back a quick acknowledgment of the message and suggested a strategy meeting the next day. She wondered why Peter had failed to call last night. Even though they had spent only one night together in the past month or so, they did try to check in with each other at least once every twenty-four hours. Esperanza was still in the Bryant Street jail. Bert was able to convince the INS people not to ship her out of the area until he could make some sense out of her legal status. Bert hoped to convince the appropriate authorities that Esperanza was a US citizen by virtue of her father's citizenship. However, the fact of Porgy's murder charge and consequent fugitive status was a tough obstacle to overcome, even if the murder charge was false. The state believed her status was that of a non-citizen and they wanted to make certain that it was their opinion that counted.

February 19, 2008

The strategy session with the other attorneys had gone well. Despite the DA's intransigence, the attorneys had gone ahead and made a formal request to file charges against the officers involved in the fatalities at the prison. They were also approaching the State Attorney General. The lawsuit was ready to file. In fact, the other two attorneys were filing the papers immediately after the meeting. Mariah was in Oakland but on her way to see Esperanza. She could tell that jail was starting to wear her down. The last time she visited, Esperanza just wanted to go back to Oaxaca and forget the whole thing. Mariah couldn't say that she blamed her.

Her phone buzzed. It was Peter.

"Hey. You able to eat some lunch?"

"Where are you at?" Mariah looked at the time. 1:30 PM. She had until 6:00 to visit Esperanza.

"By the Grand Theatre."

"I'll be there in a few minutes." She hurried out of the building next to the courthouse and walked to her car. She failed to notice the two men following her. Within five minutes she was with Peter. They ordered sandwiches and drinks.

"How you been?" asked Mariah. She reached over and touched his face.

"All right," Peter responded in kind. "Are you going to San Francisco?"

"Yeah, I gotta' check in with Esperanza. Then I'm going out to Bert's."

"I'd really like to sleep with you."

"Likewise," answered Mariah. "But Bert has an idea and he claims he needs to enact it soon." She bit into the sandwich in front of her. "You can come with."

"Maybe I will." Peter noticed two guys that looked like cops coming into the shop. It was the contractors again. The independents. They were watching him. He wasn't just being paranoid. Peter threw down twenty five dollars, grabbed Mariah's hand and left. The men tried to follow but Peter pushed the door into them, knocking one into the other. The move gave them a few seconds. Peter and Mariah ran to Peter's recently purchased car. The side window was broken. Peter unlocked the door and opened the passenger side. Mariah jumped in and they took off towards the 12th Street Bart Station. Peter found a spot to park. They left the car and ran into the station. Fifty minutes later they were in the Mission District. No one was following them. They caught a cab to the Bryant Street jail. Bert was there when they arrived. He had gained permission

to get Esperanza out under the condition she wear an
ankle bracelet and stay at his house. The three waited
for the jailer to release her.

February 22, 2008

Oakland. Downtown office building. Press conference with Mariah and two other attorneys in the Santa Rita wrongful death lawsuit.

First lawyer: Ladies and gentlemen, my name is Alexander Roberts. To my right is Attorney Al Herring and to my left is Attorney Mariah Callahan. As you know, the prisoners of Santa Rita Jail near Pleasanton, California erupted into a riot the night of July 23, 2007. The trigger for this riot remains unknown. However, the causes reside in the overcrowding, the brutality of corrections guards, and various gang rivalries between prisoners that all of California's correctional facilities feature. During the disturbance, several men who had been in one of the facility's visitors room were locked in a corridor in what was essentially a cage. These men were surrounded by chain link fencing on all sides and several guards and Alameda Sherrif's deputies. During the course of the disturbance, three of these men died. We three attorneys were hired individually by the families and friends of the deceased. After pursuing each of our cases individually, we discovered the commonality of our pursuit and started working together. The first goal we had was to determine the circumstances of the deaths. After a bit of a struggle, we were able to obtain most of the video from the jail's surveillance cameras of that night in July 2007. From viewing this video, were were able to isolate the footage that detailed these three men's deaths. Once this was done, it was quite obvious to us, the mens' families and friends, and two experts in California prison operation procedures that these men's deaths were unnecessary, wrongful and the result of gross negligence that may very well have been intentional. Once we had established this, we petitioned the Alameda County District Attorney to file charges of wrongful death and gross negligence in the pursuit of official duties against the deputies and guards involved in the deaths and their supervisors. This petition was rejected. At this time, we decided to request the California Attorney General to consider charges. We have also filed a civil suit against the men and agencies involved in the deaths. Paper copies of the suit are available to the press. It is also available on line. My colleague Mariah Callahan would like to speak now.

Hello. I just want to say that my primary goal the other attorneys at this table is justice for the families that we represent. What occurred in Santa Rita the night of July 23, 2007 was avoidable. We sincerely believe that certain individuals in the forces deployed to defend not only the surrounding community but also the men in the prison failed to do so. While some of us believe that the deaths were the result of more than negligence, it is our consensus that at the least negligence can certainly be proved. We are disappointed that the Alameda County District Attorney did not see fit to file charges against those we believe to be responsible for the deaths in that cage that night. Therefore, we believe this civil suit to be the next best option in the struggle to achieve some kind of justice for the deceased and closure for their family and friends. We are now willing to take a few questions.

Reporter 1: "Will you be making the video available to the press?

Herring: That will not be possible while the case is in litigation. Perhaps you can petition the DA's office.

Reporter 2: What about the fourth inmate who died during the riot? Is anybody representing him?

Herring: According to witnesses and the various reports of the incident, that individual was killed by fellow prisoners. His situation is being represented by the Alameda County Public Defender's office. We are not privy to any other information regarding that case.

Reporter 3: What are the chances that the California Attorney General will file charges or open a grand jury around this case?

Mariah: We prefer not to speculate on our chances.

Reporter 3: Is the civil suit a means of pressuring the Attorney General?.

Herring: We prefer not to speculate and we do not our base our actions on speculation. The lawsuit is a logical course to take no matter what the Attorney General decides.

Reporter 4: Ms. Callahan, is it true you were representing one of the men killed--Porgy Johnson--in a cold case that concerned the 1970s terrorist organization the NPLF and the murder of an undercover policewoman?

Mariah: This press conference is about this lawsuit, not about any other case. My colleagues and I have represented a number of individuals in a variety of cases and will continue to do so.

Reporter 4: You have not answered my question.

Herring: Yes, she did.

The conference ended. It was then that Mariah noticed Peter in the back of the room. She conversed with her fellow attorneys for a few minutes. They agreed to meet in a week unless the Alameda County DA or State Attorney General called one of them beforehand. Mariah closed her laptop and met Peter outside the door to the conference room.

"Hey." she kissed him. Peter squeezed her waist. "Let's get some lunch."

Casualties were down in Iraq. More civilians being killed by US raids in Afghanistan. The candidates arguing over who would be more or less bloodthirsty in the quest to maintain and expand the Empire.

Esperanza had been out of jail for a week. She was beginning to relax a little. She was still pretty pissed off. Bert had opened up his stables to her and she was spending a good deal of time with the horses. Peter's car was towed from where he and Mariah abandoned it in Oakland the day Esperanza was released. When he went to retrieve it from the lot it was impounded, he decided to leave it there. It had cost him a thousand dollars. With the damage from the day he left it and the subsequent damage from its time on the Oakland streets, he saw no point in paying another several hundred dollars to get it back. He was using public transit for the time being.

The three of them were still using throwaways. Esperanza was staying at Bert's because of her bracelet. Mariah and Peter had spent a few nights together at Peter's place, but for the most part, Mariah stayed at Bert's, too. Peter found himself spending a lot of time in the Telegraph Ave. bookstores and People's Park. The cops hadn't fucked with him since leaving him at the top of Tilden Park. He visited Nathaniel every once in a while. MaryBeth's presence on Telegraph Avenue kept him in tune with whatever street rumors there were. The street's life had changed since his days spent there. Much harder and more violent. The degree of psychosis among the street's most burnt out habitués was frightening. Yet, the culture was still vibrant and for the most part benevolent.

March 12, 2008

Herring, Roberts and Mariah had been in a conference call with a representative of the Alameda County DA's office most of the morning. The DA wanted to settle. The call had been a long negotiating session. Roberts and Herring had pretty much received what they wanted for their clients. An admission of willful negligence in the deaths. A cash settlement and the removal of the deputies directly responsible for firing the tear gas into the corridor from prison work. Those deputies' supervisors would be reassigned away from prison related duty for two years. The newspapers would be provided with the specific footage of the tear gas gun firing and the men collapsing and dying. A press conference was being scheduled for the following morning. The only clause was that all other cases regarding any of these men would be buried.

Mariah, on the other hand, was holding out. She was willing to go along with the details of the settlement, but had no intention of dropping her pursuit of justice for Porgy. She was convinced he wasn't guilty and had a statement to prove it. She was meeting with the Alameda County DA that afternoon. After lunch, she made her way to the DA's office. He was waiting.

"Ms. Callahan, please come in." He shook her hand. Two other men were in the office. One introduced himself as a supervisor in the California Bureau of Investigation. The other extended his hand and identified himself as a head agent of the FBI. Mariah took the chair offered her. The men sat down.

"Ms. Callahan, " began the FBI agent. He was a white man in his late fifties or early sixties. Dark suit and looked to be in great physical shape. Not much hair on his head. "Let me cut to the chase. You have information regarding a case that your client Mr. Johnson was awaiting trial for. That information was provided to you via extralegal means and your possession of it is potentially a crime."

Mariah said nothing. She waited for the other men to speak. Instead, the agent continued.

"As you know, the murder charge that Mr. Johnson was facing involved a law enforcement agent. What you may not realize is that that agent--Ms. McNamara--worked for several agencies. Three of them are represented here. The other agency was the Drug Enforcement Agency. You may or may not know that she was working on two very important cases when she was killed. One involved the transportation and sale of large amounts of LSD and the other involved a domestic terrorist cell that we know for certain was involved in firebombing police vehicles and may have been involved in other crimes of that nature. The FBI and the DEA were very pleased when the Oakland Police Department facilitated the capture of Mr. Johnson last year. Your assignment to his case via the public defender's office turned out to be a poor choice from our perspective, although we admire your tenacity and the thoroughness of your legal work. However, we aren't here to praise you."

Mariah waited. The guy from the CBI took over. He was a bit younger, but seemed even more no-nonsense than the FBI agent.

"We understand that you were provided some documents by a former member of our force--Richard Stevens. Those documents might implicate an individual--Mr. Freedman--in multiple crimes including Ms. McNamara's murder. As my colleague from the FBI stated, your possession of those documents could very well be a crime. However, let's assume that it isn't."

Mariah interrupted. "I don't think you have a chance of getting a conviction on any charge having to do with my having those documents in my possession."

The CBI agent continued. "Let's assume that your possession is legal. That would mean that you have proof that Mr. Freedman was an informant for at least two of the agencies represented here and that he engaged in criminal activity while being paid by those agencies for his services. However, if you have any documents that might lead a jury or judge to believe that he killed Ms. McNamara, those documents could very well be proved meaningless since they don't officially exist."

Mariah started but said nothing. She understood the game being played.

"After all," this from the FBI agent. "What we mean to say is that those documents, purported to be a confession to McNamara's murder by Freedman, have been completely expunged from all official repositories. Furthermore, any record of their existence no longer exists."

"If I released them to the press, they could take you down," said Mariah. "Or at least cause considerable embarrassment."

"And we could find some law to put you away for releasing them," threatened the FBI agent. "This is the era of the PATRIOT Act, remember."

Mariah wasn't sure about the agent's claim, but figured he was probably telling the truth.

"We have permission from our superiors," This was the Alameda County DA speaking, "to offer you a deal. Please give us a listen."

"We know that your friend Peter Somers helped Johnson flee the country back in 1980. He also served as a liaison between the various members of the NPLF. We believe he was also privy to the LSD operation Ms. McNamara was trying to take down. His knowledge could perhaps have prevented the murder of Ms. McNamara. Some of those charges could be revived and new ones added. You know this. Need I say it again--PATRIOT Act. Think of the so-called San Francisco 8."

Mariah nodded. The threats might be empty, but her knowledge of the PATRIOT Act was not what it should be. In addition, helping Porgy flee and McNamara's unsolved murder were enough to make Peter's situation tentative, at the least. She was getting angry but could do very little but listen. Her face remained expressionless.

"We are willing to forego any charges against Mr. Somers and the appropriate authorities will remove Mr. Johnson's name as a suspect in the murder of Ms. McNamara if you return any original documents and copies of those documents you may have in your possession regarding the McNamara case and the escapades of the informant Freedman. The McNamara case will return to a status of unsolved. A press release will be given to the media, including *America's Most Wanted*, that absolves Mr. Johnson of suspicion for that crime. You will sign a statement agreeing to drop the case. You will further agree to write nothing about it for public release. In addition, we will expect you to sign on to the agreement reached by your fellow attorneys and the Alameda County DA this morning regarding the fatalities at Santa Rita in July 2007."

Mariah considered her options. She didn't feel that she should make this decision on her own. "I would like some time to decide."

"You have until 10 PM this evening," answered the DA. "If you do not respond positively, files will be charged against Mr. Somers. They will be serious charges under the new terrorism laws. They are already drawn up. I can show them to you if you wish. If the name of Kathleen Soliah means anything to you, you know what we mean. Furthermore, your right to practice law in California may be suspended pending an investigation that you may have aided terrorists. I urge you to reference the recent Lynne Stewart case in New York." The other men said nothing. Mariah nodded and left.

5:00 PM March 12, 2008

Peter, Bert, Mariah and Esperanza were in Bert's kitchen. Mariah had laid out the details of her meeting with the three men from law enforcement. Peter was very angry when he heard. Not only were they fucking with Mariah's job and Porgy's name, they were trying to bust him for shit that happened a lifetime ago. But he knew the cops had the upper hand. Bert was counseling Mariah to take the deal. He told her that in cases like the one she was involved in, taking a deal was often better than fighting through the courts. Truth might not be served, but some semblance of justice could be achieved. Esperanza was just ready to go back to Oaxaca. Her experience in the United States had completely soured her. A fascist paradise was how she put it.

"Call them, Mariah," urged Peter. "It's the best for you."

"You've done well by my father," said Esperanza. "It's not worth Peter going to prison or having to go on the run and you losing your job."

Bert put in his two cents. "Essentially, they have

admitted that you were successful in your endeavor to clear Porgy's name. Their ultimatum or deal or whatever you want to call it is an admission of such." He opened a bottle of wine and poured each of them a glass. "They are now mostly concerned with covering their asses. So they are threatening you so that they can put this case back in the hole it was in before."

"Yeah." Peter raised his glass. "You did a great job."

Mariah drank her glass of wine and called the DA.

The following morning, she and Bert left early to sign the agreement. Bert served as her attorney. After the agreement was signed, he handed all the documents they had relating to Ra back to the CBI agent. Copies of all of them remained hidden somewhere in Bert's stables, just in case.

March 22, 2008

Peter, Esperanza, Mariah, Bert, Rain, Arlo, Bonita and Nathaniel were at Larry Blake's on Telegraph. Springsteen from 1975 on the sound system. "Backstreets." They had a table at the back downstairs. Esperanza was no longer braceleted. She was flying back to Oaxaca the following day. Bert had managed to get her green card restored somehow but she wanted nothing to do with the United States. Her mom was meeting her in Oaxaca.

Peter ordered a round of drinks. When they came, he raised his glass of Anchor Steam. "To everyone for their help on this fuckin' case." Glasses clinked and drinks were drunk. Mariah squeezed Peter's thigh.

Acknowledgements

I am extremely grateful to my friends and co-conspirators Marc Estrin and Donna Bister for their inclusion of this book in the launching of Fomite. Their critique and support is invaluable.

If it weren't for the multitude of people I met and knew in Berkeley, CA and the alleys bright and shadowed we found ourselves in I would not have been inspired to write this novel.

Last, but certainly not least, I wish to acknowledge my family. Their presence physically and otherwise is essential to my well-being, which is in turn essential to my writing.

Ron Jacobs is the author of **The Way the Wind Blew: A History of the Weather Underground** (Verso 1997) the novel, **Short Order Frame Up** (Mainstay 2007) and a collection of essays titled **Tripping Through the American Night**. He is a frequent contributor to Counterpunch and Dissident Voice. His articles, reviews and essays have appeared in anthologies and numerous print and online journals, including *Jungle World Berlin*, *Monthly Review*, *Vermont Times*, *Alternative Press Review* and the Olympia, WA based monthly *Works In Progress*. He currently lives in Asheville, NC and works at a library.

Fomite
Burlington, Vermont

Fomite is a literary press whose authors and artists explore the human condition -- political, cultural, personal and historical -- in poetry and prose. A fomite is a medium capable of transmitting infectious organisms from one individual to another.

≈ ≈ ≈

Loisaida by Dan Chodorokoff
Catherine, a young anarchist estranged from her parents and squatting in an abandoned building on New York's Lower East Side, is fighting with her boyfriend and conflicted about her work on an underground newspaper. She learns important lessons from her great-grandmother's tales of life in the Yiddish anarchist movement that flourished on the Lower East Side at the turn of the century.

After learning of a developer's plans to demolish a community garden, Catherine builds an alliance with a group of Puerto Rican community activists. Together they confront the confluence of politics, money, and real estate that rule Manhattan.

In this coming of age story, family saga, and political thriller, which two time National Book Award finalist Howard Norman calls an "inimitable debut novel", author Daniel Chodorkoff explores Bloch's "principle of hope", and examines how memory and imagination inform social change.

≈ ≈ ≈

When You Remember Deir Yassin by R.L Greene
When You Remember Deir Yassin is a collection of poems by R. L. Green, an American Jewish writer, on the subject of the occupation and destruction of Palestine. Green comments: "Outspoken Jewish critics of Israeli crimes against humanity have, strangely, been called "anti-Semitic" and as well as the hilariously illogical epithet "self-hating Jews." As a Jewish critic of the Israeli government, I have come to accept it these accusations as a stamp of approval and a badge of honor, signifying my own fealty to a central element of Jewish identity and ethics: one must be a lover of truth and a friend to the oppressed, and stand with the victims of tyranny, not with the tyrants, despite tribal loyalty or self-advancement. These poems were written as expressions of outrage, and of grief, and to encourage my sisters and brothers of every cultural or national grouping to speak out against injustice, to try to save Palestine, and in so doing, to reclaim for myself my own place as part of the Jewish people." The poems are offered in the original English with Arabic translations accompanying each poem.

Fomite
Burlington, Vermont

The Co-Conspirator's Tale by Ron Jacobs

There's a place where love and mistrust are never at peace; where duplicity and deceit are the universal currency. *The Co-Conspirator's Tale* takes place within this nebulous firmament. There are crimes committed by the police in the name of the law. Excess in the name of revolution. The combination leaves death in its wake and the survivors struggling to find justice in a San Francisco Bay Area noir by the author of the underground classic *The Way the Wind Blew:A History of the Weather Underground* and the novel *Short Order Frame Up*.

❞ ❞ ❞

Kasper Planet: Comix and Tragix by Peter Schumann

Graphic sedition from the director of The Bread & Puppet Theater Kasper from Persian Ghendsh-Bar carrier of **treasures** What treasures Treasures of junk Degrader of the Pre**ciou**sness system Also from India Vidushaka Also medieval subversive thrown out **of** cathedral into marketplace A midget speaking swazzel language which **cops** don't speak

❞ ❞ ❞

View Cost Extra by L.E. Smith

Views that inspire, that calm, or that terrify – all come at some cost to the viewer. In *Views Cost Extra* you will find a New Jersey high school preppy who wants to inhabit the "perfect" cowboy movie, a rural mailman disgusted with the residents of his town who wants to live with the penguins, an ailing screen writer who strikes a deal with Johnny Cash to reverse an old man's failures, an old man who ponders a young man's suicide attempt, a one-armed blind blues singer who wants to reunite with the car that took her arm on the assembly line -- and more. These stories suggest that we must pay something to live even ordinary lives.

❞ ❞ ❞

The Empty Notebook Interrogates Itself by Susan Thomas

The Empty Notebook began its life as a very literal metaphor for a few weeks of what I thought was writer's block, but was really the struggle of an eccentric persona to take over my working life. It won. And for the next three years everything I wrote came to me in

Fomite

Burlington, Vermont

the voice of the Empty Notebook, who, as the notebook began to fill itself, became rather opinionated, changed gender, alternately acted as bully and victim, had many bizarre adventures in exotic locales and developed a somewhat politically-incorrect attitude. It then began to steal the voices and forms of other poets and tried to immortalize itself in various poetry reviews. It is now thrilled to collect itself in one slim volume

❦ ❦ ❦

My God, What Have We Done? by Susan Weiss

In the summer before she is to be married, Pauline Black moves in with her boyfriend, Clifford, to test the treacherous waters of co-habitation. In the spring of 1942, Robert Oppenheimer and the Manhattan Project move into a former boys' school in Los Alamos, New Mexico to continue work on the atomic bomb. The newly-weds visit that historic site on their honeymoon, fifty years after the making of the bomb, compelled by Pauline's fascination with Op-penheimer, the soulful scientist.

The two emerging stories—of Pauline's marriage and of the devel-opment of the bomb-- reverberate back and forth, both fraught with the tensions brought on by loneliness, ambition, and secrecy. Fi-nally the years of frantic research on the bomb culminate in a stun-ning test explosion that echoes a rupture in the couple's marriage. Against the backdrop of a civilization that's out of control, Pauline begins to understand the importance of persevering in her relation-ship with Clifford.

My God, What Have We Done? pokes among the ruins left by the bomb in search of a more worthy human achievement.

❦ ❦ ❦

"The activity of art is based on the capacity of people to be in-fected by the feelings of others." Tolstoy, *What is Art?*